Also by Eleanor Wells

All Our Yesterdays

FIRST EDITION

Library of Congress Control Number: 2024926251

Ebook ISBN: 979-8-9904828-7-6
Hardcover ISBN: 979-8-9904828-8-3
Paperback ISBN: 979-8-9904828-9-0

Edited by Kaitlynn Flint
Layout by Vellum

Printed in the United States of America by Pumpkin Carriage Press, an imprint of Cinderella Pictures LLC, Boulder, Colorado.

Cover Art by Eleanor Wells

This Time Tomorrow

and other stories

Eleanor Wells

Pumpkin Carriage Press

Disclaimer

The following stories contain depictions of suicidal ideation and violence against women and children that some may find upsetting. Reader discretion is advised.

For Angela

I usually find myself among strangers because I drift here and there trying to forget the sad things that happened to me.

— F. Scott Fitzgerald

Contents

The Hitchhiker

I WAS eighteen the one time I've ever picked up a hitchhiker. The only thing between me and the void on that pitch-black November night in 1970 was the faint glow of my car's headlights.

I'd been driving nearly all day, but Denver, my old bed, and Mom's Thanksgiving cooking couldn't have felt further away. It was inching towards midnight, and I was still in the middle of nowhere when I was forced to stop for gas.

The place was a relic of my grandparents' time. I could tell from its disrepair, the damaged roof, and the wood chips speckled on the ground. Faded paint on the building's side welcomed me to historic Salida, Colorado.

I checked my map. Around 150 miles to go. Over two hours yet. My surroundings were starting to blur. All I wanted to do was sleep. I was hit with what had to be a gale-force wind as I got out. I pulled the hood of my coat over my head, only for it to be immediately blown off.

I looked back at the road. In the darkness, I couldn't see anything beyond the filling station. A part of me thought I'd cease to exist if I drove any further. I inhaled the cold air and shook my body as much as I could as I went inside to pay.

THE CLERK REMINDED me of my father; balding, a lined face with a heavy brow, and intense eyes. "Are there any hotels around here?" I asked after he took my cash.

He frowned. "What for?"

"Driving home for the holidays," I said.

"Where's home?" he asked.

"Denver."

"That's a hike, young lady."

"I lost track of time."

"You're all by yourself?" His tone was inquisitive.

"Yes," I mustered.

"We've got a spare bed. Our daughter's off at school. Would have to check with the wife, but it'd be no trouble."

He wants to murder me, I thought. *This would be a great place to get murdered. He could bury me in the woods, and no one would ever find me.* "Actually, I'll manage."

By the time my car was filled with gas, I was ready to push through the last leg.

Just as I was turning out of the station, I saw her under

the light, thumb outstretched. Her long red hair fell to her waist, and she was covered in dirt and grime. She was only using one of her backpack's straps. Her long-sleeve shirt was tattered, and she didn't have a coat.

She seemed to be about my age, but I was bad at guessing that sort of thing, so I couldn't tell for sure. Was she in trouble? How long had she been standing there? Why hadn't I seen her before? When I looked at her for another moment, I noticed the tiny marigolds printed on her shirt and something else, too.

She was pregnant.

I canceled my signal and stopped. She rushed towards the passenger side door, and I unrolled the window.

"I'm going to Denver," I said.

Without a word, she got in, dropping her backpack in the backseat.

"I'm Nell."

She nodded.

"What's your name?" I was trying to ease her nerves, even convince myself I'd made the right decision in picking her up.

"Please just drive." She spoke in a thick British accent. I caught a whiff of her body odor then and wondered when she'd last showered. I unrolled the windows and started to drive.

"No coat?" I said.

"I was in a rush."

"Rush?"

She said nothing.

"So, where exactly can I take you?"

She didn't respond.

"I'm not going to leave you on the side of the road."

"Somewhere with a phone," she said.

"I thought I saw one at the filling station," I replied.

The girl started to cry.

"I don't need to know the full story," I said, "but are you in trouble?"

She closed her eyes and leaned her head against the window.

"Can I ask..." My eyes drifted towards her baby bump, and she knew.

"He's who I'm running from."

"Did he hurt you?"

"He tried."

I swallowed, not sure of what to say. I wasn't one to pry on what was clearly a delicate situation, but I wanted to make sure that wherever she ended up, she'd be safe. "I like your shirt," I said.

"My mum had marigolds in our garden at home. I suppose it reminded me of that."

I continued to drive. "You're going to be able to call someone, right?"

The girl nodded. "My brother."

I told her I'd take her to Union Station in that case. She showed me that she had money and told me that she'd stolen it from the father of her child. Doing it, she'd been terrified but knew she'd be long gone by the time he'd notice.

My eyes drifted to the radio. "You like music?"

"I love music." She turned it on. Almost immediately, we were met with The Beatles. "Tomorrow Never Knows." Hearing John Lennon's voice was enough to light her up.

"I'm from Liverpool, you know," she said with a smile.

"Whoa, that's cool!" I exclaimed. "Did you ever see them?"

"Almost. Their last night at the Cavern. My mum stopped me from going." Tears formed in her eyes again. "What if, right?" The girl said with a sniffle.

"Right." We continued to drive, and I noticed that she kept looking back at the road behind us. "I think we're about the only cars on this road tonight," I said.

She pursed her lips.

"Is someone after you?"

"I don't think so. They're all still sleeping. I'll be in California with my brother by the time they realize."

"Who's they?"

She wasn't going to tell me. Instead, she blinked back tears as she ran her hand against her bump. "How far along are you?"

"Four months? Maybe five? Her father didn't like keeping track of the days... or me going to the doctor."

"It's a her?"

The girl nodded. "That's what they told me, last visit I had."

"I'm sure you'll be a wonderful mother," I said.

This made her smile. Not long after, she drifted off.

. . .

I woke her up once we got to Union Station.

"This is perfect," she said. "Thank you."

I shook my head. "I'm not leaving you alone."

We went in together. I waited by the phone booth as she and her brother talked, and her face went back and forth between worry and relief. After a while, she hung up the phone and greeted me with a smile.

"My brother will be waiting ."

By the time she bought the ticket, it was nearly three in the morning. The bus left at five. Her gate wasn't open yet, so she'd have to wait.

"You're sure you'll be okay?" I asked.

She nodded. "You've done enough."

"I don't mind staying if you think—"

"Nell. You've done enough. Thank you for everything."

"Okay," I said.

"By the way," the girl said. "I'm Claire."

"Claire," I repeated. "Be safe."

She took off her backpack and sat on the bench nearest us. She was shivering again, so I took off my coat and gave it to her. "Take it."

Claire looked at me with wide eyes.

"At least until you get to California," I said. "I have a few. I'll be okay."

"Thank you," she murmured.

"Mhmm."

As I turned and walked away, I watched as she put on my coat and lay down, using her backpack as a makeshift pillow.

Before I left, I called my parents. "I got lost," I told them. "I'll be there soon."

IN THE TIME THAT FOLLOWED, I thought of Claire every time I saw a marigold. I'd wonder, had I made any difference at all?

The Couple in 2B

I'm still two blocks from home when it starts to pour. Only moments before, the rain had fallen in the rhythmic sheets I've come to know all too well since I've been in London.

Oh, come on, I think. If it were warmer, getting stuck like this might have been kind of fun. Like during summer thunderstorms back home when Mom, Walt, and I would sit with blankets and pillows and watch from the safety and comfort of our screened-in front porch.

But it's only April, still early spring. The days of late have hinted at the summer to come but still carry the bite of the winter we left behind. As a chill runs through my body, I'll be surprised if I don't catch a cold. I notice the walkway, the last one separating me and my apartment, is about to change from "cross" to "do not cross."

I don't make it, and I'm forced to wait.

I sigh and catch my breath. As I do, I take in the city

streets, thinking about how mundane and ordinary it all is to me after eight months here. I try to remember what I first loved about it, what inspired me to transfer from a perfectly fine but unfulfilling existence at IU to the University of London. This place was the cultural epicenter of the world, I thought, where I needed to be. It was my Emerald City and would be my salvation. If I stayed in Indiana, I would have died before I turned twenty-one from some combination of boredom, loneliness, and exhaustion. I watch cars and the occasional passerby darting through the rain. I always thought the British had it better. They drank tea and spoke in such an elegant dialect that their problems couldn't have been severe.

I continue to wait. The rain hits my umbrella with such aggression and fervor that I'm surprised it doesn't cave in.

I'm definitely catching a cold.

If only that man hadn't stopped me when I was leaving the pub. Oh, what am I thinking? I shouldn't be mad at him. The poor guy's going through something unimaginable. His pleading voice, his desperate face, rings through my mind.

"You'll let me know if you see my Zara, won't you? She loves The Beatles and is going to be a veterinarian."

He'd handed me her picture, just in case. I'd looked at the smiling redheaded girl in a yellow dress, posing with an orange tabby cat, wishing that I had, in fact, seen Zara and could help him.

The light *finally* changes, and I can think of nothing I want more than a hot shower, fresh, dry clothes, and a cup of tea. As soon as my door is in sight, the light of my apartment beckoning, I dash. Too fast. Before I know it, I'm lying face down on the wet concrete. I've definitely scraped something, and I'm aware my bag and its contents have scattered nearby. I sigh.

Doing swell, Nat, I think. I'm about to find my way to a stand when I hear a woman's pristine, kind voice.

"You all right, miss?"

"Fine." I look up. I see the woman. Honey-blonde hair in waves, her aquamarine raincoat shining in the moonlight. Her boyfriend had already started gathering the fallen items from my bag. Built with a mop-top of dark hair, he looks like he walked out of a London Fog catalog.

I stand up wearily, just as the boyfriend finished collecting my stuff. "Long shift at the pub," I say. "Ready for a hot shower and maybe a cup of tea."

"You're our neighbor, aren't you?" the woman asks.

I nod, realizing it's *them*. The couple from 2B. I don't know what their names are. Oh no. Ever since I moved into 2C, I've been partly fascinated, partly afraid of these two. I've seen it, observed it. The kisses, the lingering glances, the beginnings and ends of date nights. They're young, beautiful, and in love, all any of us could ever want. I feel like a wet sock standing next to them.

"Chloe," she says, extending her hand.

I take it.

"Malcolm," says the boyfriend.

"Natalie," I say tiredly.

Malcolm already has his keys, so I walk behind them.

Inside, as I readjust to the warmth, I know I'm flustered. Malcolm and Chloe are already whispering to themselves. I've been forgotten in an instant. Maybe I am a wet sock.

We get to the second floor, and I take a left to 2c, them a right to 2b.

"Good night, Natalie," Malcolm says.

Gosh, I love the way he says my name. "Night," I call back.

I realize something's wrong.

My keys aren't in my bag.

I could have sworn I locked behind me when I left for work.

I toss everything out and back in.

The picture of Zara, the missing girl, gets torn in half in the struggle.

I sigh, knocking three times in all, each louder than the last. No one answers. I remember that Nancy was visiting her family in Brighton this weekend, but of course, Lynn was gone too. I check under the mat. No spare. Lynn must have forgotten to put it back again. I don't know for sure, but I don't care. All I know is that I'm wet and cold and probably bleeding underneath my pant leg.

I feel Chloe's eyes on me.

"I'm locked out," I say with an exhausted huff. "I don't think my room—sorry, my flatmates, are home."

"Oh, you sweet thing," Chloe says.

After a pause, Malcolm puts his hand on Chloe's shoulder. "You're free to wait with us," he interjects.

"Are you sure?"

"It's no trouble at all," Chloe says. "We were going to heat up some roast beef if you're hungry."

I agree since I didn't have a chance to eat much at the pub, it being Friday night and all. I follow them in.

Their apartment is gorgeously decorated, with a bright red shag carpet in the center of the living room. I recognize a reprint of Picasso's *Les Demoiselles d'Avignon* above their TV and record player.

I've always liked this one because each of the women depicted in it all have stories to tell. To some, they might just be naked prostitutes, but I've always thought there was more to it. How did they get there? What are they thinking and feeling?

"I love the painting," I say. "I like art."

"Are you an artist yourself?" Chloe asks.

"Just an admirer," I explain. "I'm studying journalism at the University of London. I'd like to do it for music. You guys have all the great bands. So, I had to come here."

The two smile as I shiver in my wet and dirty clothes.

As Malcolm says he'll help me lay out my things to dry, Chloe notices me shivering and asks if I want to use their shower.

"Yes, please."

She gives me one of her pajama sets to borrow and helps me get set up in the shower.

Miraculously, I'm not bleeding, but my knee is

scraped, and there will probably be a fresh bruise in the morning. I write my fall off as a warning to be more careful and look where I'm going like my parents have always told me. I turn up the water temperature as high as it goes for me to still be comfortable, washing away the troubles of the day.

The man's voice from the pub rings in my ears again, calling out for his daughter. I try not to pay attention to the news because it bothers me too much. Every day, there's another murder or car crash or a new stat about how many people have died in Vietnam. I still get sick if I think too hard about Sylvia Likens.

Zara isn't the only girl that's gone missing. Five teenagers have vanished in the last nine months, walking home from school, sports practice, or fun with friends, never to be seen again. They found two bodies in the last week, buried in shallow graves near the famous White Cliffs of Dover.

I fear the worst for Zara and the other kids who haven't been found.

I hear Chloe and Malcolm's voices from down the hall, though I don't hear what they say. It starts off like sweet nothings and seems to get tense. I figure all is okay, that these are the normal kinds of conversations that couples have. I wouldn't know. I've always been alone.

I dry off. As I put on Chloe's pajamas, the impossibly soft fabric caresses my skin. They must be silk. I check the tags. They are. They hang on me loosely, like they don't belong. I stare at my reflection. The bathroom light brings out every vein and imperfection in my pasty skin. I'd cut my mousy brown hair to my ears earlier in the year because Lynn told me that a bob would bring out what she called the "rich color" of my eyes. It didn't quite work out the way I'd been hoping. I know I have to start carrying myself with more confidence, but that's easier said than done when everyone walks by you without a second glance.

I sigh and splash water on my face.

When I leave the bathroom, I'm greeted by the wonderful smell of roast beef and potatoes. They've laid out a place for me at the dining table. The candle they burn in the center creates a relaxing ambiance. I see my things lying out on towels as I sit down.

"I can't believe I'm so clumsy," I tell them with a slight laugh.

Chloe and Malcolm wave me off. "We're happy we were there to help," Chloe says.

As we eat, the conversation continues. They ask me if it's hard being so far away from family.

"Sometimes," I say, even though there's nothing waiting for me in Indianapolis. Ever since Walt started a family of his own, we don't connect. With Mom and Dad, all I'm doing is holding onto a memory of my past and childhood that I know I can never get back.

They tell me about *Bonnie and Clyde*, the movie they just came from.

"I haven't seen it yet," I tell them, "but Warren Beatty? After *Splendor in the Grass,* I'll watch him in anything."

Chloe blushes.

"She loves Warren Beatty," Malcolm says.

I watch as they turn to each other, sharing a smile and a quick kiss. Next, Chloe asks if it's all right if they put on a record.

I nod.

"What are your favorite groups, Natalie?" She asks.

"The Rolling Stones," I say immediately.

"Favorite member?" Malcolm asks.

"Brian Jones," I say as redness floods my cheeks. I don't tell them about the picture of Brian I have taped close to my bed.

"Correct choice," Malcolm replies.

As Chloe goes to start the music, Malcolm turns back to me. I wonder why I was afraid of them for so long. Something about them feels safe. It's so natural, too. I'd tried to befriend Nancy and Lynn when I moved in, and they always rebuffed me until I got the hint.

"Paint It, Black" fills the air, preceding a stretch of silence. My eyes turn to my stuff, and the photo of Zara, ripped in half. They see me looking.

"Awful about these kids going missing," I say. "That girl, her dad was at the pub, just hoping someone knew something." They keep looking at me, so I continue. "I think she was walking home from school, and it was broad daylight. Scary, huh?" They continue to stare at me silently.

"Yes," Chloe says, and the conversation awkwardly fades.

I shouldn't have brought it up. I remind myself that not everyone likes randomly talking about these kinds of things, and now I've made them uncomfortable.

As we finish dinner, Malcolm asks if I want to stay for a drink. Maybe it's fine, and I didn't creep them out as much as I thought. Before I can answer, though, the rain stops, and I suddenly remember why I'm here in the first place. Lynn has to come home at some point. I just need her to let me in, as I'm pretty sure my key is hanging on its hook in our front hall. I should probably let her know where I am.

I tell this to Chloe and Malcolm. I asked to borrow a pen, piece of paper and tape so I could leave a note on the door.

What follows is a very long stretch of silence, and I'm not sure if I've done something wrong. Finally, Malcolm says, "Alright. But promise you'll stay and have a drink with us. Your stuff isn't even dry."

I agree. He gets up from the table and returns a moment later with what I asked for. I'm aware of Malcolm watching me as I scrawl a quick note. It unnerves me in a way I can't quite explain. But I'm on edge now.

I tell them I'll be right back.

In the hall, I catch eyes with Lynn. "Hey," I say, folding up the paper in my hands. "I'm locked out. Do you know if I left my keys inside?"

Lynn shrugs. "I don't know."

"The couple in 2B's helping me out. Mind waiting for a sec? I just want to grab my stuff."

"Okay..."

I know I promised Chloe and Malcolm a drink, but now that I have a way back into my apartment, all I want to do is sleep. I look down to 2B, then back at Lynn. Something possesses me to ask her to follow.

She agrees.

I've left the door cracked open, and Lynn waits as I go inside. Malcolm and Chloe have moved from the dining table to the sofa, and they have a drink set out for me. "My roommate's back, so I'm actually going to go," I say. "I'm sorry. But she's waiting outside in the hall now."

"We made this for you. Don't be rude," Chloe says, her tone now clipped. There's a twinge of anger to it.

"I'm sorry," I repeat, "but it's been a long day. Thank you so much for dinner and for the help. I really do appreciate it." If I wasn't so tired and Lynn wasn't waiting outside, maybe I would have stayed. But I was already fantasizing about my bed.

Without a word, Chloe stands up and starts shoving my things into my purse. She hands it to me a moment later, her smile all but faded. Malcolm's glaring at me, too. I hesitate for a moment, knowing I've messed up, but I don't think there's any fixing this tonight. I leave, thinking I'll apologize the next time I see them around.

LYNN DOES HAVE THE SPARE. She gives it to me to keep until my keys turn up or I can get them replaced. I spend the next twenty minutes trying to find them, but they're nowhere in sight.

A few minutes before I give up, I realize I'm still wearing Chloe's pajamas. I'll make a point to stop by sometime in the morning so I can give them back and get my other clothes from them, too. Maybe they'll have seen my keys.

THE NEXT MORNING, I'm making tea and spreading jam on a piece of toast. I actually hear birds chirping outside. It's supposed to be a nice day. I'm off from both work and class, so I plan to treasure it. Maybe I'll treat myself to the movies and see *Bonnie and Clyde*.

I'd tried looking for my keys again when I woke up, but nothing surfaced.

As soon as I take my first bite of toast, I hear what sounds like a stampede right outside the door.

I wonder what it could be. It sounds like the police. Slowly and carefully, I walk closer to the door. They pass right by us and stop at 2B.

My heart starts pounding.

A moment later, Lynn joins me in the hall. She's just woken up. "What's going on?"

"No clue," I say. "Police here."

Lynn moves past me and opens the door. I see a few officers crowding the door. One, a gruff, muscular one, apparently the leader, is pounding at the door.

"Police, open up," he yells.

Lynn and I stand frozen as Chloe opens the door and starts talking to them. They push their way inside. Lynn closes the door and looks to me. "Weren't you there last night?"

I nod. "I wonder what's up."

"Probably drugs," she says with a shrug. Lynn goes into the kitchen, and I follow a moment later to finish eating my breakfast.

It wasn't drugs. It's about two and a half hours later, and I've been sprawled out on the couch and watching *The Avengers* when I hear a knock at the door.

Curious and a little scared, I go to open it.

It's one of the officers, a younger one whose name I forget as quickly as he says it. "Natalie Miller?" he asks.

I nod.

He asks if I can come down to the station for questioning.

"Questioning?" I ask.

"Eve Parker, Beatrice Green, William Johnson, Portia Black, Zara Kincaid," the officer says. "Do those names mean anything to you?"

Kincaid. That was Zara's last name. I remember it because her father had introduced himself as Tom Kincaid. The others are the other missing teenagers. "I met Zara's father yesterday," I say.

"Please, Ms. Miller, come with us."

I tell the officer I need to get dressed. He waits, telling me he'll drive. I ask if I'm in trouble. He refuses to answer.

Of course, I'm not in trouble. I haven't done anything. But I still feel like I'm going to collapse.

AT THE STATION, I lose track of time. I'm ushered into a room where two detectives, an older man and a younger woman, wait for me. I quickly realize the man is good cop, the woman, bad. Even though they tell me their real names, I call them Winston Churchill and Jane Asher. Everything is a blur as Churchill starts asking me how well I know Chloe Dearborn and Malcolm Wallace.

"Not well," I say. "They helped me last night when I lost my keys."

They ask about ten times if I ever spent any time at their apartment other than the night before.

Why were my clothes at Chloe and Malcolm's place? Why did I have a set of her pajamas?

I explain again and again.

"What about your Stones records?" asks Jane.

"*My* Stones records?" I ask, confused.

"Ms. Dearborn said you were letting her borrow them," she clarifies.

"Those aren't mine," I say, my tone defensive and angry.

They ask about Zara, about Portia, William, Beatrice, and Eve, what I know about them, and what I've heard. They ask why I have Zara's picture. I explain.

After an indeterminate amount of time, Jane leaves and Churchill looks to me and says, "you know we found your keys in their flat?"

What?

"No... I..." I trail off. "They let me in because I didn't have my keys. Malcolm left all my stuff from my purse out to dry—"

"Miss Miller," says Churchill calmly. "We found the bodies of William Johnson and Eve Parker last week, as you may or may not know. We have reason to suspect that Ms. Dearborn and Mr. Wallace are responsible. They're being detained. We're trying to get to the bottom of this."

"I don't know anything about that," I say, my face pale.

Churchill gives me an empathetic look. After I answer a few more questions, I collect my keys and the outfit I left behind, and he lets me go home.

IN THE FOLLOWING DAYS, the police find Beatrice, Portia, and Zara near the White Cliffs where they found Eve and William. Chloe and Malcolm both confess. As details emerge and they're charged with five counts of murder, I try to make sense of the night I spent with them, bonding about the Stones and Warren Beatty and Picasso. But I can't.

Nearly a year passes, and they go on trial.

Chloe is accused of luring the kids into her car under false pretenses, using her charm and beauty to gain their trust. She'd take them back to the flat, where Malcolm would be waiting. They'd gain their victims' trust, drug them, and kill them. They're convicted and sentenced to life a short time later.

How had I never known? How had I never seen anything?

They'd been very insistent on me having a drink with them. What was in it? Was I going to be next? Why had Malcolm taken my keys and lied to me about it? What had he been planning to do with them?

The Babylon Girls

Rose Mason envisioned the day millions of eyes would be on her as looking very different. She'd be in a gorgeous dress on the Academy Awards stage, holding her Best Director Oscar and thanking everyone who had always believed in her.

Not in a courtroom, on the witness stand, and running on less than two hours of sleep as cameras, lawyers, and spectators tried to decide whether or not her demure nature was genuine.

Rose fidgeted in the cheap button-down blazer and skirt she'd bought from Goodwill the night before as she tried to look anywhere but at Will. His gaze was the most piercing; he could have killed her with a look.

Her shirt scratched against the back of her neck.

She'd never cut the tags.

The prosecutor, a tall, lanky man with gray hair,

spoke. "Ms. Mason, please state your full name for the record."

"Rose Deanna Mason."

"Do you recognize the defendant?"

"Yes."

"Can you point him out and describe what he's wearing?"

She did so.

"Ms. Mason, to the best of your ability, tell us your recollection of the events of November 16th and 17th, 2015."

THE AFTERNOON of November 16th had been a cold and frosty one as Rose sat at the Babylon Café. She'd been anxiously pushing a peppermint mocha back and forth between her left hand and her right, trying to think of what to say to Will and berating herself for ever getting involved with him in the first place.

Rose checked her phone. It was 3:15, and she'd been waiting for forty-five minutes. She'd texted Will a simple "here" once she'd gotten a table, and he hadn't replied. After waiting ten minutes, she'd sent a follow-up.

> By window.

He had yet to text her back. She set her phone down and sighed, cupping her face in her hands to try and stop crying.

Rose looked up and saw a girl with shoulder-length

brown hair, blue eyes and a friendly smile looking at her from the next table over. The textbook in front of her was thick, highlighted, and tabbed to death. She'd seen this girl here before, always studying, though Rose thought she must have been from another school.

"Let me guess. A guy?"

It took Rose a moment to realize the girl was talking to her. She nodded vaguely.

"It always is." The girl sighed, took a sip of her drink, and locked her eyes on Rose. "He isn't worth it, and you're going to be okay."

"You don't even know me," Rose said.

The girl gave her a look. Something between understanding and pity. She turned back to her studying then. Their conversation was over.

As Rose took a few anxious sips of her remaining mocha, she didn't realize it was possible for time to move this slowly. When she checked her phone again, it was 3:20. He wasn't coming. Of course, he wasn't. Maybe a part of him knew, and that's why he wasn't showing up.

Never break up with someone over text had always been the advice. She was doing what you were supposed to do, and it was biting her in the butt. She wasn't going to wait anymore. She wanted to get back to her dorm before it got dark. Will may have escaped this conversation today, but he wasn't going to forever.

Rose stood up, feeling the girl watching her as she put on her coat.

She started crying as soon as she left the Babylon,

wrapping her scarf up to her eyes and pulling her hat down as far as possible so that no one would notice. She wished the events of the week before hadn't happened so that she could go on pretending everything was perfect.

"AND YOU WERE aware the woman you spoke to was Ms. Hill?"

"At the time, I was not," Rose said.

"And were you aware that Ms. Hill and the defendant were romantically involved?"

"I was not," Rose repeated.

"Please tell us how you met the defendant."

IT HAD BEEN a peaceful Friday afternoon at the beginning of May. Rose sat in the Babylon Café, facing the window, her turkey sandwich untouched on her plate. Her first year of college was nearly done. She'd had to abandon any illusions that it would be her salvation. In high school, she'd daydreamed constantly about the friends she'd meet, the adventures she'd have, and the missing fulfillment she'd find.

The sun was peeking through the clouds. How long would it last? Twenty minutes? Fifteen? Rose could never be sure.

She thought about the summer ahead. Earlier in the year, she'd made the conscious choice that she would not be going back to Green Bay. It had taken her eighteen years to get out of her mother's house, and she knew, if she went back, she would only backslide.

She'd started to second guess her plans the moment she acquired a summer job at the Field Museum. Thinking about navigating three months of isolation in the city made her ache for the familiarity of home. Still, everything was already done; the deposit on her sublet paid, the job officially accepted. It was going forward no matter what.

Rose often thought that she was meant to live a lonely life. She knew the pervasive emptiness of her day to day made her writing good. Still, she couldn't escape the feeling that spending her time with things that didn't happen to people that didn't exist was a poor substitute for something real.

She saw the boy in the bomber jacket eyeing her then, his blond hair neatly coiffed behind his ears. Rose straightened her posture, fixed her bangs. The boy's eyes stayed on her as she took another bite of her overpriced sandwich. The bread was dry, and the pepper jack cheese didn't even have a kick. She wouldn't have leftovers. She wondered what it must be like to not have to have buyer's remorse about a sandwich.

The boy was still watching her. Rose realized she'd seen him around school.

"Has anyone ever told you you look like Joni Mitchell?"

Rose sat up with a start and realized the boy was beside her, a to-go bag in hand, intently regarding her. His cheeks flushed as his mouth curled into a nervous smile. "I didn't mean to scare you."

"It's okay," Rose whispered. She got lost for a moment in his eyes. They were gray. She didn't know if she'd ever met someone with gray eyes before. "To answer your question, yes." Once, years earlier, a friend of her mom's, whose name she couldn't remember, had made the comparison.

"Do you, by chance, go to Columbia?"

Rose nodded.

"I thought you looked familiar." He took a seat next to her, extending his hand. "I'm Will."

"Rose."

Then, he asked her to dinner. She didn't know that this was something boys still did. They exchanged numbers and set a date for that Sunday.

Rose spent the entire weekend convinced that she was about to wake up from a dream.

But it wasn't a dream. It was real life. It was as if she'd been holding her breath for her entire life. After that Sunday night, she could release it.

It made that summer much more bearable, exciting, even.

As Rose walked, she tried to think of where exactly things had gone wrong. A blissful first month of dating had led to them seeing plays at the Steppenwolf and Agnes Varda movies at The Music Box. Over the Fourth of July weekend, the two had gone up to Lake Geneva.

The adjustment to the new school year had been okay.

She'd first suspected he'd been cheating in those few weeks. She'd felt the change, him growing distant, the arguments about petty things. He constantly told her how beautiful she was without backing up his words with actions.

The texts—to and from someone named Cailey—had been the final straw. Will had forgotten his phone at her place. It wasn't like she'd gone snooping for anything. It had been right there, plain as day, on his screen.

> I miss your face.

She'd gone through their message history, and there was no mistaking it.

As soon as Rose got back to her dorm, she thanked God she was alone. Hopefully, Lucy was with John, and she'd have the entire night.

She checked her phone again. Nothing. She was about to call when she saw three dots appear on her screen. Gripping her phone tightly, she waited as the dots danced back and forth, disappearing for one moment only to reappear the next. She waited seven minutes in all. His text arrived at 4:13 p.m.

> Hey - I'm SO sorry. I got held up with studying and then my phone died and I forgot my charger at home. I just got here but I don't see you?

Rose took a minute to catch her breath. Then, she typed a reply.

> I waited for almost an hour, so I left.
> Call me tomorrow when you get the
> chance. Goodnight, Will.

A moment later, she texted him again.

> Actually, no, don't bother. I'm
> breaking up with you. I saw the
> texts between you and Cailey, and
> frankly, I'm past the point of
> wanting to hear your explanation.

She put her phone on airplane mode, flopped onto her bed, and screamed into her pillow.

That night, Rose had one of the worst nights of sleep of her entire life, drifting in and out of consciousness. She'd waited for nineteen years to find someone who wanted to date her, and now, she was going to be alone again. But it wasn't just that. The words of the girl she'd spoken to at the Babylon looped through her mind.

He isn't worth it, and you're going to be okay.

Rose was standing up for herself. She wasn't going to settle for less because she was afraid to be alone. Maybe she was going to be okay.

She woke up from a dream at 4:47 a.m. to find it was still pitch black. She'd been standing at the edge of a dock, about to board a ship that she sensed would take her away from all of her problems.

"OBJECTION, RELEVANCE," came the defense lawyer.

"Your honor, Ms. Mason is using the dream to explain

that she was clued into the fact that something was wrong."

"I'll allow it," said the judge, a man Rose sensed was grandfatherly to those he liked but stern with anyone who crossed his path. He turned to her. "Continue, Ms. Mason."

IN ROSE'S DREAM, the wind assaulted her from every angle as she spoke to the captain. He informed her that the journey was going to be rough and unpleasant, but if she didn't leave now, it would be unclear when she would get another opportunity.

As she sat up in bed, an eerie feeling washed over her. It was something that she couldn't describe beyond the sense that she felt as though she'd exited the world she knew and entered into another one. Something was different now, something that she couldn't explain.

She starkly remembered the text she'd sent Will and stalled as long as possible before summoning all of her courage to take her phone off airplane mode.

It took a few minutes for everything to trickle through. First came her emails. Then, news and weather. And then, all of Will's messages. There were 36 texts, 28 missed calls, and 11 voicemails in all.

She'd go to the texts first so as not to overwhelm herself. Rose glanced out her window. In the daytime, you could see a simple view of the Chicago streets; now, there was only the faint illumination from streetlights. This time of the morning always gave Rose an otherworldly feeling, like she didn't exist at all.

As she read through everything, it all processed on a delay.

There was nothing before 9:42 p.m., when the first missed calls and texts came through, followed in quick succession by several more.

> Rose, baby, please pick up the phone.
>
> I don't even know why you're mad at me.
>
> Please call me back.

At 10:07 p.m., the voicemails started rolling in.

Rose was so delirious from the tonal whiplash of the past week that she only half heard them. None of them made much sense. He was evidently outside as she could hear the winter wind muffling variations of "please just talk to me." He sounded drunk. He told her that he was scared.

At some point, Rose put her phone away and squeezed her eyes shut. She'd never even had a chance to confront him about Cailey. If he loved her as much as he claimed he did, then why was he cheating on her?

All that she knew was that she didn't want to talk to him ever again.

Rose awoke again a few hours later and checked her

phone. Will hadn't texted her after the "I love you" at
4:13 a.m.

She'd deal with it later. She had class in less than an hour.

Somehow, she found the energy to get out of bed and
get dressed, and try to go about her day.

Writing the Short Film had almost been remarkable in
its normalcy. Thankfully, it was her only class of the day.
Afterwards, she caught up on studying in the library and
went to an on-campus screening of *White Christmas*.
Briefly, she forgot about Will, about everything.

She'd been through the end of the world and no one
had a clue. Maybe all it meant was that the girl at the
Babylon was right.

She was going to be okay.

After, Rose went to the common area to make herself
dinner when she saw Lucy there, doing the same. "Hey,"
Rose said.

Lucy raised her eyebrows. "Oh," she said. "Hey."

"How's it going?" Rose asked, her tone cheerful as she
laid out peanut butter, jelly, bread, and a plate on the
counter. Couldn't go wrong with a PB&J.

"Oh…" Lucy started. "You don't know."

Rose had just dipped her knife into the jar of peanut
butter. "I don't know what?"

"Your boyfriend was arrested."

Everything froze. Arrested for what? Rose intuitively
felt that this was related to the phone calls, but she struggled to make the connection. He'd been outside. Public

indecency, maybe. She couldn't stop the questions that came out of her mouth. "When?"

"It's like a developing story, but... a girl's body was found... it's... in *The Chicago Tribune*..." Lucy trailed off, took her phone, and showed it to Rose.

ROOSEVELT STUDENT FOUND DEAD IN GRANT PARK, SUSPECT IN CUSTODY: BREAKING

Rose read through, managing to absorb the important details. In the early hours of the morning, a maintenance worker had found the girl's body. She was quickly identified as Cailey Hill, a junior at Roosevelt, and an English major. She loved sports, crafts, and traveling. She wanted to teach Creative Writing one day. Rose started shaking profusely as soon as she saw Cailey's picture. It was the girl from the Babylon.

Her roommates had reported her missing when she failed to return home from studying. They told the police to look into her on-again, off-again boyfriend, Columbia senior William Fleck. Sure enough, witnesses had seen them leaving the Babylon together. They'd found him in short order at his apartment.

Everything clicked at once. Not only was Cailey the one she'd talked to at the Babylon, but it was the same Cailey whose texts she'd seen. Still, nothing made any sense. She dropped the phone.

"Sorry..."

Lucy picked it up. "Don't worry," she said, concerned.

The voicemails, Rose thought. She left, leaving her unmade dinner sitting on the counter.

Somehow, she found her way to her bed before she collapsed. So much was coming into focus. Why he always came to her. Why she'd never met anyone in his life. Did anyone even know about her?

She found her way to her phone again, and only made it one voicemail in before she couldn't do it anymore. She tried to listen and find out if she heard anyone else. No. No one but him and the winter wind. If this was true, Cailey must have died before he called her the first time. But he sounded too calm.

Will was a lot of things, but capable of murder? No, he couldn't be. These voicemails were evidence of something, at least. A day passed, and then two, and no one reached out to Rose. It was all Will and Cailey and how it had been love at first sight.

After a week, Rose went to the police.

"But you didn't just go to the police," said the defense lawyer on cross. "You visited the defendant in jail, didn't you?"

"Yes," Rose said meekly.

"And why did you do that?" he demanded.

"I wanted to know if it was true."

. . .

She lied that she was his sister.

It was a bitterly frigid afternoon when she sat in the jail, everything cold and sterile. She was convinced she'd made a mistake and wanted to turn back, but it was too late. Rose's heart could have stopped as two guards brought him out. Seeing him in the orange jumpsuit made her realize the gravity of what had happened, what he'd allegedly done. Still, she wanted something, any confirmation to tell her this wasn't true. He hadn't done this. He hadn't killed a person, and she wasn't the other woman.

"I had a feeling it was you," Will said quietly. He looked tired, worn, pathetic. How had she ever been attracted to him?

Rose had to catch her breath. "That day you left your phone, I saw the texts between you and Cailey."

Will pursed his lips.

"That's why I wanted to meet you that day," she continued.

He said nothing.

"So, is it true?" Rose asked.

"No," Will said defensively.

"Are you sure?"

"Rose," Will said. "I'm sorry I was late. I…"

"Did Cailey know about me?"

Will's face went white.

"You were cheating…" Rose trailed off, reminding herself of why she was here. Pretending this was only about cheating could only do so much for her now.

Will opened his mouth but could only stumble over his words.

"Did she know?"

Rose saw the scenario in her head. Him showing up at the Babylon. Them talking. Leaving together. Something about why he was upset, why he was there. Had they gotten into a fight about something? About Rose?

"Well, *did she*?"

"No," Will said, his face even whiter. "This is all a misunderstanding."

Rose scoffed. "They said you left with her."

"It means a lot that you would visit," Will said after a long silence.

She took a good look at him. His gray eyes were cold. There was no light in them at all.

She still didn't understand what was happening, but she knew she needed to tell the police about the voicemails.

It would change her life forever, but she'd never be able to live with herself if she didn't.

The night following her testimony, Rose dreamed of Cailey. They were at the Babylon, except it was spring. Sunny, serene. They were laughing and talking about something.

"Rose, we have a lot in common," Cailey said to her. "I think we're going to be great friends."

Daisy Bell

After years of telling everyone she knew that she was going to start a garden, Cassie finally planted her first flower at the age of twenty-nine, in the first few months she'd been back in the Midwest.

It had been so easy, driving the mile and a half to the plant shop, picking out the seeds, and making her transaction. She wondered why it had taken her so long and why she'd wasted so many excuses on not doing the thing she knew would bring her joy.

Yellow daisies had been her pick.

Yellow had always been her favorite color, and Daisy had almost been her name. They'd been her first favorite flower when she was four years old, which she'd proudly demonstrated over and over again on all of her crayon drawings.

Teaching acting classes had been nice, but lately, a

thought had been starting to creep into her mind that she wasn't going to progress. It was that very thing that had made her determined to leave her hometown to begin with.

Yet, Los Angeles wasn't what she was looking for. The older she got, the more Cassie doubted that there was a world where she could exist as a creative. She'd never even be able to rent a house with a yard in LA and live alone. What if she'd stuck it out? Would things be much different?

She covered the seeds with dirt, forgetting about all of that for a moment. Now, to wait.

Cassie wiped a bead of sweat from her forehead, closed her eyes, and let the moment linger. Before she could blink, summer would be over, and she needed to remember what it was like to get her through the winter months. She felt her bare knees against the grass and dirt and sweat pooling from underneath her old drama shirt. She'd have to shower and chuck her clothes into the dirty laundry as soon as she went inside. Maybe this was what would make her happy. No audiobook narrations of best-selling novels. This. She was about to stand up when a man's soft voice called in her direction.

"Cassie?!"

The voice was immediately familiar, though she couldn't quite think of why. She turned and saw the source: a man with tufts of reddish-brown hair and a slouched posture. He wore a red polo, khaki shorts, and tennis shoes. Where had she seen him before?

He approached. "I'm sorry. I hope I'm not interrupting anything."

Cassie shook her head.

"I'm Sam Michelson," he said.

She still drew a blank.

"We went to high school together?"

At that moment, it clicked. "Yes, hi," she said with an embarrassed smile. "How are you?"

Sam didn't answer the question and instead turned the focus back to her. "I listened to—"

"*Yellow Canyon*?"

He nodded.

Cassie lit up. "Yeah, it's actually the first time an audio version's been made. I don't know if you know, but Talia Granger—"

"Was a recluse? Anyway, they were waiting for your voice."

He flashed a grin that twinged with something Cassie thought was a flirt. No, it couldn't be. They'd only been in school together a year, and that had been so long ago.

She hadn't said anything when he added, "You should have been Marianne. In the movie."

"Well, I was a little too young when it was made—"

"When they do a remake, they'll get you to play the part," he said, once again cutting her off.

Cassie blushed. "Well, I voiced her, so."

Sam's body awkwardly shifted from left to right. "You wouldn't want to go out sometime, would you?"

Cassie pursed her lips. "No, probably not."

Sam threw up his hand. "No worries," he said with a wry, embarrassed look. "Have a good day."

He'd already walked away before she had the chance to process the interaction. She rubbed her eyes and sighed.

Straight to that.

Nothing in between.

She sighed and did her best to move on with her day.

Cassie hadn't thought about Sam Michelson since senior year of high school. After the odd interaction, decades-old memories returned to her with startling clarity. He'd been in tech during the spring production of *Les Mis*. She'd been Cosette.

Not only that, but they were in film club together. Still, when he wasn't goofing off with his freshman friends, there were a lot of quiet stares, and at one point, someone said to her, "He totally has a crush on you." But she'd thought he had a girlfriend who'd also done the show. What was her name? It started with a V. Vanessa? Victoria? No, Violet.

Another thought spun through Cassie's mind. Sam hadn't seemed all that surprised to run into her. Almost as if he'd been expecting it.

You're crazy, she thought to herself. *Just forget about it.*

THE FOLLOWING DAY, Cassie's mother had planned to have a cookout. She'd sent her daughter at least ten messages in the preceding week, mostly about what to buy. Ketchup or Mustard? Brioche or pretzel buns? What kind of beer did she drink these days? Cookies or brownies for dessert? Her mother had retired the year before and, ever since, had found ways to keep herself busy. Gardening was one. Cooking was another. Providing for her daughter now that she was home was the last. Cassie still hadn't gotten the hang of cooking in the way that she should have a long time ago now. There had never been time or money or opportunity. Now, since she was back and had the time and quiet, what she lacked was motivation.

She was thinking about all of this as she walked to her car after work. Another long-buried memory emerged. One day in film club, they'd watched *2001: A Space Odyssey*. Mr. Whitnall, the teacher, who was thirty-five and Cassie had a crush on, had asked them why Hal did what he did.

"They were going to disconnect him," Cassie said. "He was protecting himself."

Mr. Whitnall looked at her then, the intensity of his blue eyes cutting through her. "So, would you say that Hal had some level of humanity? After all, he feared death."

Cassie paused in reflection. "Well, no. He killed all those astronauts and didn't care."

"Do you think he knew it was wrong?" Mr. Whitnall asked.

Sam, sitting in the back, answered for her. "He was doing what was best for the mission. So, if you blame anyone, blame his programmers."

By then, they were out of time, and Mr. Whitnall had left them with a parting thought. "I'd like you all to think not only about how this film applies to your own lives, but what consciousness is. See you next week."

Suddenly, Cassie realized she was standing idly in front of her car. There was a single daisy on her dash. Had it fallen? No—it was too delicately placed. It had to have been put there.

She tossed it in the grass.

Weird.

Five days passed with Cassie impatiently waiting for when her daisies were going to bloom. They'd told her ten to twenty days at the shop. And yet, as she passed by her empty garden plot, she second-guessed herself. Had she done something wrong? Were they ever going to sprout?

She sighed and went inside.

SAM WAS at the bagel place the following morning, where she'd gone to grab breakfast before work.

It had a name, Rhiannon's, but everyone called it the bagel place. She'd been sitting on an old-fashioned wood bench, waiting for her food, when she'd heard his voice call her name. He'd just ordered, too. "Hey, Cassie."

"Hey," she said.

Before she could react further, he'd slid next to her. His face was inches from hers as they sat there. She felt boxed in, like she had nowhere to go. "So, why *did* you move back here?" he asked.

"Long story."

"I've got time."

His hand moved in an unmistakable fashion down her thigh, making the hairs on her skin rise.

His smile grew wider as her heart started thumping. Her salvation came in the calling of her name.

"Sorry, I don't." She stood up and avoided his gaze, and the crestfallen look she imagined was on his face.

On her way to work, she realized she'd wanted to ask him if he lived or worked in the same area. That would explain why she'd run into him twice in the last week. But maybe the fact that she'd forgotten meant that it didn't matter.

It was another day before she saw the daisies on her dash. This time, it was a bouquet, and there was a note. Cassie's hands shook as she opened the crumpled piece of notebook paper.

> Hey Cassie,
>
> I wanted to apologize for how abrupt everything was yesterday and the awkwardness of the first time I ran into you. Maybe that's why you threw my flowers away? Anyway, I never thought you'd come back here. I guess I've always liked you. Well, loved you. If you gave me a chance,

I could take care of you, of us. My dad died last year, and there's still enough from his inheritance for a down payment on a house. Even enough for one on Lake Drive like you always wanted.

By the way, I get your decision to move away and live the simple life. I think you probably saw that people aren't authentic out there and wanted something real. I respect you for that. But you're too good to be teaching. Let me take care of you. I have a job, too, and a good one. I'm on track to make six figures by the end of the year.

Think about it. I have a funny feeling destiny brought you back here, to me.

Sam

Incredibly, he'd left his number at the end of it.

She neatly folded the paper, then crumpled it in her fist. At first, she didn't know what the Lake Drive part of the note was referring to.

Then, she remembered.

In high school, she'd often tell others how nice it would be to live in a mansion on Lake Drive. She'd always passed it off as a joke, but there was a genuine seed to it all.

That was over ten years ago.

Cassie swallowed. This had to end right now.

She typed his number into her phone and sent him a text.

> Hey. I got your note and the
> flowers. Thank you so much. I am
> not interested. Please have a good
> one. - Cassie

He immediately started typing. She waited for a minute or so.

After another, still typing.

She threw the flowers on the ground.

For the entirety of the fifteen-minute drive, she was so nervous it took everything she had to keep her eyes on the road.

As soon as she pulled into her driveway, she yanked the phone right out of the charger so hard she felt like something was going to break.

She saw his response.

> ok. Sorry to bother you.

Cassie sighed and deleted the text history. Eventually, she managed to get out of her car and walk down the narrow path towards home.

The daisies still hadn't sprouted yet.

That night, she lay in bed, thinking, once again, about senior year.

He'd been sitting alone during dinner break on their

two-show day of *Les Mis*, so she'd gotten her plate of pizza and sat next to him. "Where's Violet?"

"She broke up with me," he said.

"Do you want to talk about it?"

Sam shook his head, sniffling. "Don't you have other friends?"

"I see them all the time," Cassie said, "and I don't think anyone should have to eat alone."

She didn't even remember what they'd talked about. But she'd done her good deed, graduated, and moved on with her life.

Now, this.

THE NEXT MORNING, Cassie's mother, perhaps intuitively sensing that something was off, invited her over for dinner. She agreed without hesitation.

They ate outside. While it was still July, and there would be plenty more warm evenings before the inevitable chill of winter in the Midwest, everyone was always aware of how fleeting the season was. So it was always spent outside.

And it was a beautiful night. The crickets gently chirped as Cassie laid her bare feet in the grass, looking down at the chipped red polish on her toes. As the taste of smoked sausage melted on her tongue, it reminded her of how things used to be and a time in her life when there was nothing ahead of her but her dreams. In her mind, she'd meet the love of her life by 21, have an Oscar by 24, married with a kid on the way, and living in the Holly-wood Hills by now. Instead she was facing down the barrel of thirty with no sense of where her life was going or if any of it had meant anything at all. There had been short films, plays, and extra work dotted throughout her soul-sucking office job and rejections so severe that she wondered what the point of living even was.

Yellow Canyon had given Cassie a glimmer of hope, as it had come into her life when she was about ready to give up on acting altogether. She'd read the book in high school and it had come and gone in within the limited perspec-tive of her teenage mind. But, as an adult, she couldn't have related more to Marianne. It can only take so much for someone to snap and realize they don't want to partici-pate in society anymore. It had kept her going for a while, and then, it all faded away like it had never existed.

Her thoughts drifted to Sam, the flowers, and the note. She'd kept her phone off since the afternoon, and finally, she had the courage to turn it back on.

Once her phone booted up, she immediately saw countless dings. Two were texts from Sam.

> It's really too bad.

Moments after that came:

> I'm sorry I didn't see that you're just another blonde bimbo. Have you had plastic surgery? Either way, Hollywood changed you.

Minutes later came one from Instagram.

hal24601 tagged you in a post.
"@cassiedouglasactor ruins Talia
Granger's…"

Cassie shut off her phone and looked right at her mother. "Sorry."

"What's wrong?" her mother asked, concerned.

All Cassie could manage was a pained look.

"Work?"

Cassie shook her head. Her mother had no idea. She squeezed the phone in her hands and slid it off to the side. "I ran into someone I used to go to school with."

"Oh? Who?"

"No one you knew," Cassie said. "But I guess he had a crush on me or something. He asked me on a date."

"In high school?"

"No. Now."

"And what did you say?" her mother asked with a raised eyebrow.

"I turned him down," Cassie said dryly. She had a moment to consider her next words when she started heaving, thinking about all the texts and how she didn't look for fear there might be more. That had been really stupid of her to text him back. She burst into tears.

Her mother instantly came over to her chair and wrapped Cassie in her arms. "Sweetheart, what is it?"

Limply, she managed to show her mother their message history. "He's been leaving flowers on my car…"

After her mother's advice to block his number, they changed the subject.

LATER THAT NIGHT, when she was getting ready for bed, she noticed her missing underwear. Her bras had been messed with, too. Was she going crazy? She'd combed through the house, still filled with boxes. Beyond that, nothing else had been taken.

She looked at the post she'd been tagged in then, the one she knew was from Sam. It was a public one-star review of the *Yellow Canyon* audiobook. She sighed and shut off her phone. Was this all he had?

She always kept everything locked. Maybe she was imagining things because she was already on high alert.

Still, she deadbolted everything and drank herself into a stupor. She needed to forget.

IT WASN'T QUITE four in the morning when she rose with the intuitive feeling that something was off.

Shaking, she reached for her phone.

A second after the harsh glow cut through the darkness, she saw the texts on her screen. All from an unknown number.

Do you really not remember?

Let me refresh your memory.

Sam had taken a picture of a playbill. Cassie swallowed as she realized what this was. It was the production of *1984* where she'd played Julia. There was the note in her handwriting. "Sam! Please stay sweet and kind. Love, Cassie. Go Cobras!" With it, he'd texted:

> December 2019. The Los Feliz
> playhouse.

Cassie's phone shook in her hands as she started, then deleted the beginning of a response about five times.

Before she could think of what to say came another text.

> I see you typing.

She noticed the missed calls then. Dozens of them. Finally, she thought of what to say.

> Have you been inside my house?

It wasn't a moment before she got her answer.

> You keep your spare key under
> your mat.

As she released her phone onto the end table, the darkness felt all-consuming. She was so alone, and she was scared. Another ding.

> I loved you like no one else ever
> will.

And another.

Come outside.

There was a loud, unmistakable knock at the door.

"Cassie!" he cried. "Please just talk to me!"

Maybe because it was four in the morning and she had no one or nothing else, she went. She grabbed a kitchen knife, though. In the faint moonlight, she noticed his eyes were streaked with tears. He was hunched over and wearing tattered clothes. He saw her knife first. "I'm not going to hurt you," he said.

After a long, pleading look, her grasp on it loosened, though it remained in her hand. "You need to leave me alone," she said. "Otherwise, I'll call the police." It was a vague threat since she had little faith they would do anything.

"I need to explain."

"There's nothing to explain," Cassie said, continuing to point the knife at his throat.

"You were the one person who was always nice to me and who made me believe the world was a good place," he said. Carefully, with his left hand, he took the signed 1984 playbill out of his pocket and handed it to Cassie. "I was really depressed on that trip and I was going to kill myself and I saw you in the play and I couldn't believe it." He sniffled.

Cassie gazed at the note as he continued.

"You gave me enough hope to keep going that day."

She said nothing.

"You've always given me hope."

In spite of everything, looking into his sad, pleading eyes, she pitied him.

"And if I can't have you, I don't know what the point of living is."

"Come on." She noticed then that his fist was balled around something covered by his sweatshirt sleeve.

It all happened fast.

He lunged toward her. The gun he'd been concealing went off, and the bullet barely missed her. In another flash, she plunged the knife into his chest. She heard it all: the gurgling, the light leaving his eyes. She let go and called for help as soon as he dropped the gun and collapsed on the ground.

Sam Michelson, age twenty-five, was pronounced dead at the hospital some hours later. She'd stabbed him right in the heart, so it would have been fruitless no matter how quickly the police had gotten there.

He'd been in love with her since the day she'd sat next to him in *Les Mis*, maybe even before that.

Because of the circumstances—about as cut and dry self-defense as you could get—she was expected to go on with her life. But everything had changed in that early morning.

That afternoon, her daisies finally bloomed.

End of the Century

THE END of the eighties coincided with Janet's senior year of college. The start of 1990 would mean the century itself was almost over, and there was a greater than zero chance that humanity would be gone by then. 2000 didn't seem like it could be a real year that humans could live in, or so Janet thought.

It was the beginning of October when Robby caught her after class and asked if he could walk her somewhere. She'd had a crush ever since the start of the school year. He was her type: long, dark hair covering his eyes, skinny frame, punk fashion. Her own Joey Ramone. She thought he felt it, too, as his eyes often lingered on her from across the lecture hall.

In spite of Olivia and Heather telling her it was only a matter of time before they hooked up, they had yet to exchange more than a stray word here and there. Until that afternoon.

"Do you like Halloween?" Robby asked as leaves crunched beneath their feet.

Janet paused, taking in the scene around her. From a distance, the quad—red, orange, and yellow as far as the eye could see—was punctuated with jack o'lanterns. The buildings themselves had paper witches, ghosts, and scarecrows taped to their windows. Come summer, she'd go back to California, and perfect Plimpton, New Hampshire autumns like this one would soon be a memory.

"Janet?" Robby repeated.

"Oh yeah. I love it," Janet lied. There was something about the holiday that always gave her the chills. She could barely handle scary movies. She knew Heather felt the same, but Olivia lived for this time of year.

"Good, because I'm having a party. You and your friends should come," he said, managing a smile.

"Okay, we're in," she said.

"Right on. It's Halloween night. I'll tell you where."

The tingle of arousal spread through her body as they continued to walk.

"Hey, you're from California, right?" he asked.

She nodded.

"So, fun fact. I'm sure you know about the Greene cottage? It's on Maple Street, just up the road."

Janet nodded. She knew of the crime but not much else.

"Yeah, this couple that was murdered there in the forties? The son hid under the bed, and now he's this freak who supposedly lives up there. Some kids disappeared in—"

"1969?" Janet said. Olivia had told her the story of the Nashua Five at the start of freshman year.

"Anyway, there are rumors they ran into the son, maybe ended up at the house? I've always wanted to check it out, but..."

"You're too scared?" Janet teased.

"No!"

They both laughed. Her body tingled again as he put his hand on her back.

"Anyway, I'm this way," said Robby, pointing left.

"And I'm that way," Janet replied, pointing in the other direction.

Their eyes stayed on each other for a moment. There was something deeper to this feeling, something different. It was desire but with an added layer.

I want to get to know you.

She watched him walk out of her line of sight. Then, she took her Walkman out of her bag, letting Joey Ramone's voice drown out the rest of the world as she made a stop.

At the library, Janet pieced the case together through faded newspaper clippings.

One of the first headlines was "PLIMPTON COUPLE FOUND DEAD." Below it was a grainy black and white photo of a man in a plaid hunting jacket, wearing a vacant expression, his arm around a woman in a fur coat. Janet was confused for a split second before realizing this was

Roger and Celia Greene. She'd never known what they'd looked like. These days, they were more urban legends than people who actually lived.

Celia had a son from a previous marriage. Wayne was his name. Whether or not he still lived there, nobody knew.

On that frosty October night in 1947, he'd been awoken by the sound of his mother's screams. Then he'd hid under the bed. His aunt had come by with breakfast that morning. It had been so cold that there was a layer of frost on the ground when she saw their mangled bodies. There'd been so much blood in their bedroom that no one would have guessed their bedsheets were originally white.

The police found Wayne still under his bed, frozen like ice.

He went to live with his aunt and uncle in New York before eventually coming back to New Hampshire. In 1969, five friends from Nashua went missing. They'd last been sighted at a grocery store in Plimpton, talking to a man who matched Wayne's description. But nothing ever came of it, and their bodies were never found.

"It's kind of weird, don't you think?" Heather said that night over cheap pizza, stale beer, and the scent of marijuana smoke. "People died. It's not Disneyland."

"We'll just go and see it. We won't go *in*. Come on, it'll be fun."

Olivia set down her beer and looked Janet in the eye.

"Who are you, and what have you done with Janet Sullivan?" She gestured to Janet's dark pixie cut. "Cutting off all your hair, and now this?"

"I don't know," Janet said quietly. "I guess I've been thinking about how fast time goes."

THOUGHTS of the Greenes spun through Janet's mind in the weeks leading up to Halloween. Celia and Roger had been a perfect couple. They'd met volunteering on a scrap metal drive. Wayne's father had died before he was born, drafted into World War II. Roger was Celia's second chance at love, and the three of them had an idyllic life in their cottage on Maple Street until it was all abruptly ripped away. It seemed unfathomable that they'd never caught the person who'd done it. It had been long enough since the crime that only a select few remembered what the town was like before.

As she passed through each day—all different, yet all the same—Janet couldn't shake the feeling that she was biding her time. Everything, from her classes to the partying and the meaningless sex, was a distraction from the inevitable. It wasn't like she had much to look forward to, anyway. She'd always been mediocre, too mediocre to do anything meaningful with her English degree. Besides, picturing herself after college only ever brought back a black, empty void.

"Where do you see yourself in five years?" Teachers,

counselors, and employers would ask. The truth was, she
didn't.

Anyway, what did it matter? It never seemed to make
sense to Janet that everyone lived for the future when they
all could be dead tomorrow. Even her relationship with her
two closest friends wasn't the same, mostly because they
were playing at the absurd notion that they'd all keep in
touch after graduation. It was like high school all over again.

On October 30th, the girls smoked weed and watched
It's the Great Pumpkin, Charlie Brown on TV. Their
costumes were set. They'd be the three Heathers from the
movie—Janet, Heather Duke, Olivia, Heather McNamara,
and Heather would be Heather Chandler. When they
were figuring out what to do, Olivia had complained the
group costume was incomplete because they didn't have a
Veronica. Heather just said, "Come on, humor me."

THE GIRLS STOPPED at a liquor store first. The elderly
clerk flirted with Heather and she'd flirted back as he
asked who they were all supposed to be. Only Janet bore a
resemblance to Shannen Doherty. Heather and Olivia
didn't look like their characters in the slightest.

Because Janet was the designated driver, Heather and
Olivia passed a flask back and forth.

"Don't worry," Olivia said from the backseat. "You and
Robby will be plenty warm tonight."

Redness flooded into Janet's cheeks. "Come on."

"You know we're right," Heather teased.

"Unless you're saving yourself for Joey Ramone," Olivia said with a mischievous grin.

"Shut up," Janet said, her face bright red.

Olivia started playfully laughing, and Janet had to tell them to stop so she could focus.

They were about to turn onto Maple Street.

It was so dark that the girls wondered if they were in the right place. Then, they saw it hand-printed on the mailbox. Greene. Janet saw the dirt path snaking up the hill leading to the cottage.

Not a single light was on.

Away from streetlights and underneath the faint glow of the moon, this must have been exactly what the street was like in the forties. The crickets. The leaves rustling in the wind. Some things never changed.

"Are you *sure* this is it?" Olivia asked.

In answer to their question, they saw a figure walking towards them. He was tall, muscular, and square jawed. His sandy hair was streaked with gray. He wore a red plaid shirt and jeans. The man smelled of pine needles and woodsmoke as he approached.

Fuck.

"Can I help you girls?"

"Yeah, we're lost," Janet said. The lie was so half-baked she knew he didn't believe her.

"Where are you trying to go?" He asked.

"Downtown," she answered, continuing her lie. "We took a wrong turn."

"I imagine you three have got places to go, people to see," he said.

"Well—" Janet started.

"If you girls aren't in a rush, I was about to get a fire started. And there's hot apple cider on the stove."

"Well, I wouldn't mind a hot drink while you gave us directions," Janet said.

"Sounds like a plan," he said with a smile. He extended his hand to Janet first. "I'm Wayne."

As the three introduced themselves, his gaze was completely fixed on her. He was attracted to her. She wondered if he was imagining what her body looked like underneath her turquoise blazer and plaid skirt.

"Are you supposed to be Paul Bunyan?" Heather said flirtatiously.

"No, this is me every day," he said wryly.

Janet inhaled. This was him. Celia Greene's son.

A chill ran down Janet's spine as she, Heather, and Olivia exchanged a look of hesitation. It would be okay. He was kind, warm, and friendly. It was to be expected that, considering his circumstances, he'd be a bit socially awkward. It wasn't like any of them could ever understand how undergoing such a tragedy—and so young—could affect you.

"Well, I'm a terrible host," Wayne said, gesturing up the hill. "It's up this way."

True to his word, he'd begun setting up the kindling for a bonfire and wiped off leaves from the splinted wood benches that surrounded the pit. As he adjusted the precise positioning of branches and old cardboard, Olivia wobbled on her seat. She nearly fell but caught herself as Wayne went to steady it. Heather scooted over so Olivia could join her.

"I need to get those replaced," Wayne said. "Those are the same ones I sat on as a kid. But it's hard to let go."

"I can imagine," Olivia replied.

Janet was shivering profusely. It wasn't a very cold night, but all she could think of was how nice the fire would feel. Wayne looked at her, concerned. "You okay?"

"Just cold," she managed.

"She's the designated driver," said Heather, "so *we're* doing great."

Wayne gave them a look. "Who wants cider?"

"Yes, please," Janet said.

Olivia and Heather also agreed to a cup.

"There's no booze," he warned.

"No worries," said Heather with a plastered grin.

He looked back at the pit. "Roger taught me how to build fires. It's all about the methodology." After a moment, he took a match and set it ablaze, illuminating their surroundings orange. He beamed them a smile and went inside to get the cider.

Once he was out of earshot, Heather leaned into Janet and Olivia. "Okay, this place officially gives me the creeps."

"Why? He's harmless," Janet said.

"Are you sure?" Heather challenged. "What if he killed those people twenty years ago?"

No one said anything.

Wayne came back a moment later with the cider. As they talked, Janet was pretty sure he asked what they studied, how they'd all ended up in Plimpton, and that he was awfully uncurious about why they were really there.

Sitting and watching the dancing flames, Janet thought that this was the first time she'd felt alive in months.

Then she remembered feeling very tired.

THE ROOM WAS warm and smelled of cinnamon. Janet's head throbbed as she realized she was lying in a bed, dressed in a scratchy, withered beige nightgown. Instinctively, she knew. This had belonged to Celia.

She was in a bedroom, lost in time. There was a poster of Lou Gehrig facing her, hanging above a wooden horse that looked at least fifty years old on the dresser. Beside it was a signed baseball.

She tried to scream but couldn't. Duct tape covered her mouth. She tried to move, but her wrists and ankles were bound to the bed with rope. Still, she tried to sit up. Her body was lead. A blunt pain hit her pelvis as she did, and the gag meant she couldn't scream.

A moment later, she heard footsteps.

It was Wayne, of course. He eyed her and knelt down, stroking her forehead.

Janet shrank back.

"Sshhh," he whispered.

There was blood on his hands.

Fresh blood.

"Those ridiculous costumes were getting on my nerves." He didn't elaborate further. Instead, he changed the subject. "I'm not an idiot."

Janet tried to speak, but it was muffled by the duct tape.

"I'll take it off soon, but first, you need to let me talk."

She relaxed.

"My stepfather was in a lot of debt. He had a little operation on this property, growing... They called it reefer in those days. It was no grand scheme, their deaths. Just a fucking drug hit."

He took her gag off. She caught her breath and then cried, "What do me and my friends have to do with it?"

"You wanted to come and see the place where my parents were murdered. It's been forty-two years, and you kids never learn your lesson."

"I—"

"No, honey, there's no excuse."

"Where am I?"

"You're in my room," Wayne said. "I know you didn't mean to hurt me, and that's why I'm giving you a chance."

"What did you do to my friends?"

He didn't answer. "Here's what we're going to do. "Your car is right where you left it. And whoever finds the keys first gets to leave."

"But—" she started.

"No questions," he said, untying her binds.

Then, he left.

What... the ... fuck.

Everything moved in suspended animation.

Janet somehow managed her way to a seat, thinking about the blood on his hands, the blood that now caked her forehead. She wobbled up to a stand, groaning from another sharp pain that hit her pelvis. She wasn't wearing underwear under the nightgown. Her upper thighs were bruised.

The second she swung open the door, it clicked. She was in a time capsule. Every intricate detail—from the wallpaper, the curtains, the furniture, the radio where a TV should be—was perfect. It all seemed familiar, and she realized this wasn't an ordinary time capsule; she recognized this living room under the sheen of heavily filtered black-and-white crime scene photos. He'd redone everything in exactly the way they'd been in 1947.

She'd admire it if the circumstances were different.

Janet paused and tried to listen. It wasn't a big house. So she had to hear someone somewhere. Instead, there was nothing but crickets, creaky floorboards, and the wind from outside.

Somehow, Janet put one foot in front of the other, not sure where she was going or what she was looking for, as she slowly tiptoed through the hall.

"Heather? Olivia?" Her voice croaked as thirst overtook her. How long had she been out? What had he given her? Had he—

Her thoughts were cut short by Olivia's scream from

the end of the hall. Janet knew what was coming, what awaited her, but she knew what she needed to do.

The door was already wide open.

There was so much blood in the master bedroom that Janet only recognized Heather from her curled red hair and the costume she'd come here in. Olivia stood beside her, still alive. The key was right there, in Heather's hand.

Olivia was hyperventilating and shaking as she noticed Janet and let out a blood-curdling scream.

"Get away from me! This is all your fault!"

"Like I knew he was a psycho," Janet said. All her fault. Right. Like they hadn't leaped at the chance to do it.

Olivia screamed again. "Oh my God! Why are you so calm?!" She snatched the keys from Heather's limp hand. "Are you coming or what?"

Janet's blank stare was enough answer for Olivia, who darted down the hall.

Another scream as she heard a gasp and then a thud.

Janet stepped into the hall, watching as blood and drool gurgled from Olivia's mouth. They locked eyes as she tried to stand, only to collapse a moment later. The keys fell onto the floor, and she took her last breath.

Towering above her was Wayne. He wiped blood from his mouth and tossed the axe aside.

The stench of death was quickly overwhelming the house. "You're different from them."

Janet scoffed. "Why? It was my idea to come—"

He took a step forward.

"—because I wanted to impress a guy."

She looked past Wayne down the hall. It was too risky to try and take the keys, she thought. How far were they away from town? Two, maybe three miles? It had been so short in the car, but late at night, in nothing but a nightgown, it seemed insurmountable.

He took another step and flinched. "My God! At least put up a fight!"

Again, she looked at the keys, the hall, and the front door. Even if she did make it back, then what?

Tell the world she'd gotten her friends killed?

She felt his hands, gargantuan, against her shoulders. Her head smacked against the doorframe as she fell. She had enough strength left to run her fingers through her hair. Blood.

Robby's party was probably going on. Janet thought of it: the cheap beer, loud music, drugs, dancing and laughing with other people her age as she tried to soak in the last of her college days. Those were the kinds of bad decisions you were supposed to make in your early twenties. Maybe that was what she needed all along. Not this.

Normalcy.

What on earth had she been thinking?

She thought of her childhood bedroom, the Ramones poster facing her bed, and the lemon tree in her backyard. Goldie would come and snuggle with her in the hammock as she read. She'd been a good, sweet dog...

Wayne grabbed her and shoved her against the wall.

What would happen now?

Would anyone ever find them?

Would she ever be remembered?

Robby would find someone else. He'd marry her, cut his hair, get some office job, and have a nice, quiet life. Maybe, someday, he'd tell his kids about the girl he used to know.

What would happen to Wayne? How long had he been like this? Had he killed the Nashua Five, too, or was it all a horrible coincidence?

Did he ever have a chance with the hand he'd been dealt?

Janet had the faintest vision of the newspaper headline. "PLIMPTON COLLEGE THREE STILL MISSING," it would say. They'd probably use her driver's license picture for the photo. She wasn't sure about Olivia or Heather.

The more she thought about it, the more it all made sense. There was a reason things were blank after college. It was always meant to end like this. It just happened sooner than she thought.

Again, against the wall.

She tasted chocolate. Brown sugar.

It was a memory.

Her mother's cookies.

There'd been one afternoon when Janet had been about eleven, laying out and reading with Goldie under her arm.

"Come on and get them fresh out of the oven," her mother said. "But wash your hands first."

Where She Came From

Mom and I are in the dining room. Outside, it still snows, though the blizzard seems to have stopped. It's only November, and winter is already here.

I twirl noodles around my fork and take a bite, peanut and udon dissolving in my mouth as the scent of pine from a Bath and Body Works candle wafts from the next room. There's a lull in our conversation. Now's the time to say something.

I impulsively picked him from the list for our sociology final. I didn't want anyone else to pick him. I doubted any one of my classmates, none of whom could place our city on a map, could do it justice.

"Freya?" Mom says. For a moment I think she's caught onto the fact that there's something I want to say. Instead, she just asks, "did the noodles turn out?"

I nod. "Yes."

"Are they spicy enough?"

"Perfect," I say.

"Let me know if there are any other recipes you want me to make while you're here," Mom continues. "I'm going to the store tomorrow."

I nod and take a deep breath. It's now or never. I watch her nod in acknowledgment as I tell her about the sociology project and how I'm doing it on him.

"Okay," she says.

"I was wondering, well—" It was so long ago that she last told me about her friend. Since I didn't remember his name, I thought I could figure it out by looking at a list of his victims. But I didn't. There was always the most about the first, the kid, and the one who'd escaped. Everyone else was just footnotes. "What was your friend's name? The one, you know..." Even though she knows what's coming, I can't bring myself to say it.

"Hector Alvarez."

"Is there anything else you can tell me?"

"Like what?" Mom asks plainly.

"What do you remember... about when the news first broke?"

"I was in Spain," Mom says. "Anyways... his..." she trails off. "Freya, can we not talk about this right now? Please?"

"Okay," I say quietly. "No problem."

I have one week. One week of being here to put together as much firsthand information as I can.

That night, as I'm lying in bed beneath endless layers

of blankets, I find a documentary about him on YouTube to listen to as I try and fail to fall asleep.

I was born two years after he was arrested and sentenced to life, and only a year after he was killed in prison. In high school, the reality of who he was and what he'd done, that it affected real people, would hit me in the most brazen of ways. Passing a mall here, a store there.

This is where it happened.

This is where he picked up men.

Being attracted to them was his only prerequisite. More often than not that meant not being white. That meant the police weren't in a hurry to figure out what had happened to you.

For my entire life, his name and face have been a boogeyman.

And yet, there's so much I don't know. There's a lot that a lot of people don't know, even if they think they do.

About halfway through the two-hour video, they say Hector's name. He was the eighth, twenty years old when he died.

"On December 8th, 1986, he'd kill Hector Alvarez after meeting him at the Moonrise Rollerway..."

I look at the video on my phone screen. By then they've already moved onto the next victim. I have to rewind it, to the grainy, faded black and white picture. Hector's mouth forms a tight line as his hair is slicked back.

I close my eyes and try to see him as he was. Not this one picture, but living, breathing.

Next, I look up the Moonrise Rollerway. It still exists. I've lived my entire life in this city and I've never heard of it.

It's on the other side of town. Maybe I'll go tomorrow.

I close my eyes as I turn the video back on and finish listening.

Mom leaves for work by 7:30. I catch her in the hallway on her way out just as I've woken up.

"There's coffee and an egg bake on the stove," she says.

I thank her and ask if she's ever heard of the Moonrise Rollerway.

"Of course," Mom says as if offended that I'm even asking. "Man, I used to go there... well, in college."

"Is that where you—"

"Is that where I..."

I take a moment and catch my breath. "Did you ever go with Hector?"

"In college," Mom says. "And yeah, he and I went a few times."

I nod as Mom gestures towards the front door. "See you tonight."

I watch as she leaves, and I am alone in the house.

The weather forecasts a high of ten degrees, but sunny. The cold snap will be gone by Thanksgiving, but it makes everything around me feel strangely ominous. The same kind of ominous that drove me away in the first place.

I know if I want to go to the rink I'm going to have to take the bus. It won't be fun in the cold, but I'll live.

It takes an hour and two transfers to get to the other side of town. After an agonizing twenty-five minute wait where I wrapped my scarf tight around my head and tried to think as many warm thoughts as possible, I board the bus, noticing an older woman in the very back, her gaze fixed squarely out the window. I wonder about her, about what she's seen, what she knows. She was around when he was. Without a doubt.

Mom didn't have a car for most of her early adulthood, not until she met Dad. She took the bus everywhere, even in the dead of winter.

I see her in the center of the back row, except it's summer. She wears a mint green blouse and acid-wash jeans. A knit bag is slung over her shoulder. Her skin is sun-kissed, and her brown hair falls in waves to her waist. She's beautiful, so beautiful that I wonder why she didn't pass down more of her genetics to me. She won a beauty contest when she was nineteen, and I'm me. I've seen pictures of her at this age, but I've never been able to escape the dissociative feeling that the woman was someone else. My mother could have never been that young. She's distant, though. She stares straight ahead, right past me. Towards what, I don't know.

I hear Hector before I see him. "Odie," his voice calls. I recently learned that she almost exclusively went by Odie when she was young. When she came back from Spain was when she decided to start going by Odette. You have to listen carefully to hear his Mexican accent, but it's there. I see him past the filter of black and white, living, breathing. He's handsome too, his dark hair in a mullet, dressed in a cream-colored shirt and dark pants. A red backpack is at his side. It's the 1980s, without a doubt.

Mom breaks from her haze and looks up at him. "What?"

"Are you okay?" he asks.

Mom takes a deep breath. "I guess I'm still thinking about that missing persons thing that we saw. That shit gets to me, you know?"

Hector gives her a reassuring look. "All you can do is pray for them."

"Yeah." She looks back at Hector. He gives her a goofy smile, getting her to smile too, and eventually, she does.

"Hey," he says. "What do you think they're going to play?"

"My husband, Donny Osmond, duh."

They disappear, and I realize I'm about to miss my first transfer.

As I STEP inside the Moonrise Rollerway, I wonder how I made it my entire life without ever hearing about it.

It's frozen in time, this place. I see the echoes of what it once was in the faded paint and broken neon.

I wish I could go back.

I've been thinking this a lot lately, about why I have to live in this time when I am so much more interested in what came before. Why is it impossible to even get a chance to try it out?

In my first freshman seminar, they told us that history gives us the ability to look forward. For me, I see it as always trying to capture the intangible fog of something I know I will never be a part of.

I can only imagine what our city must have been before he desecrated it.

I've only ever lived in his shadow. Maybe he's only one small part of our story. But, if I have to be honest with myself, what else have we contributed to the world that's instantly recognizable by just about anyone?

It's him, his name, and all it represents.

An upbeat pop song I don't recognize blasts as I watch a ghost rink, and for a moment, I see it alive, vibrant once more.

"Can I help you, sweetheart?" The man's voice takes me back. Gregarious, he wears a football jersey, and I realize the game is on. I look down at my sweatshirt and turtleneck combo and realize I've dressed in our team's colors. I'm okay with him thinking it was purposeful. Even though I left this city ages ago and have no plans to live here ever again, any time I visit, being here always makes me want to fit in.

I wasn't going to skate, but I find myself paying the fee and rental nonetheless. Maybe loosening up is what I need.

When was the last time I roller-skated? When I was a kid? When I had the world ahead of me, and anything was possible?

I finish tying up my laces as David Bowie's voice propels me onto the rink.

I start slow at first. I wobble a few times but catch myself. I'm gliding when I see Mom and Hector again. They're skating to the same song. Mom was a gymnast and a figure skater. I might look like a fish flopping on dry land, but for her, it's effortless.

Eventually, she twirls into Hector's arms. He catches her, puts his arms on her shoulders, and they stare into each other's eyes. They're stopped, their faces very close, but they won't go any further than that.

"I'm going to miss you when I'm gone," Mom says.

"I'm not going anywhere," Hector replies.

"I wish international calls weren't so fucking expensive—"

"Odie. You're going to have a life to live. Adventures to go on. Don't worry about me."

They decide to get food at the café, and I do the same.

I devour a burger and fries that are surprisingly good, but I don't know if it's the quality of the food or the fact that I'm desperate for something hot. There's something about the red and white tiled floor and dark ceiling with cartoon-like stars that makes me feel like I'm not in the real world.

Mom and Hector are a few seats away, in regular shoes now, their bags at their side. Between bites, he unzips his backpack and takes out a worn book. *La Caseta Mágica. The Phantom Tollbooth.* My heart pounds as I watch.

"Feliz cumpelaños y navidad," he says. *Happy Birthday and Merry Christmas.*

Mom takes the book, her eyes wide. "Hector..."

"Tú eres una gran amiga," he says. *You are a great friend.*

"Thank you," Mom says, hugging him.

"Promise me you'll read it," he tells her. "When you get back, you can judge the translation."

"I will."

Suddenly, I'm not at the rink anymore, but I'm fifteen. It's spring, and I'm lying in my bedroom. Mom had given me her copy of the Spanish translation a few years before so I could practice. It was mine, I thought, mine to do whatever I wanted. So when we were cleaning out to donate, I put it in one of the bags.

Mom pounds on my door. "Freya." She doesn't wait for me to respond before she opens the door. Her face is filled with rage. She holds the book. "I can't believe you."

"Why? What?"

"Why would you give my book away?"

"I..."

"Why would you do this without asking me?!" Mom yells.

"I'm sorry, I thought it was mine!" I find myself on the defensive now, not sure what I did wrong.

"No! It's not! I gave it to you to borrow!"

"Three years ago?!"

"Ask first. Are you really that selfish?!" She slams the door and leaves.

Back to the rink, but it's winter now. Hector is at the cafe, alone, watching people skate. It's busy. Nearly every table is full.

He is there, too. Tall, chiseled face, blond hair around his brow and ears. He's muscular, well dressed. There's no dancing around the fact that he's handsome. He walks with a stiff gait, his shoulders slightly slouched. I wonder if it was endearing that someone so handsome could be so uncomfortable in their own skin.

He and Hector lock eyes, and he waves.

Hector waves back.

He sits.

I can't hear anything.

Because, in real life, no one did.

All anyone knows for certain is that Hector left with him that day and was never seen alive again.

My phone dings, taking me back.

Mom's texted me.

U still at Moonrise?

I tell her yes, and she says she can pick me up. She's on this side of town, and her afternoon client canceled.

I meet Mom in the parking lot about fifteen minutes later. As I get in the car, she's regarding the building.

"Brings back memories," she says. "I used to come here all the time."

"Yeah, I... my paper, you know."

"Yep," Mom says, starting to drive. "When's it due?"

"The outline, not until next week, but I..." There's so

much more I want to say, but Mom's mostly shut me down when it comes to talking about him, and I never know what is too much. "I'm thinking about my angle. For the paper. I want to do justice to all the victims and make sure it's not a hundred pages long."

Mom laughs. She actually laughs. I find myself smiling as she gets serious again. "Hector was the one that got me that copy of *The Phantom Tollbooth*. I'd been talking about wanting to read more in Spanish, and it was my favorite book to read when I was little. I have no idea how he found it, but he did."

I nod.

"If you need me to look anything over, let me know."

"Sure."

As we drive, I watch the almost bare trees pass by, fallen autumn leaves caked with snow. The sun is low in the sky. I used to hate this time of year, especially here. I still do, but I have to admit that it's beautiful.

"Freya?"

I turn my head.

"Chinese takeout tonight?"

"That sounds great."

Princess in the Tower

I WISH I didn't remember my past. If it had all happened when I was, say, two or three instead of seven, I might have been able to pretend that this had always been my life and that my name was really Madeline. Sometimes, my past life came to me in dreams. At other points, it hit me like a ton of bricks at the most random of times. Whenever it did, I always think about how I should have died on that summer night in 1999, and how I've been living on borrowed time since then.

Once, it happened at the Farmers Market, while I was helping a customer. Rebecca had the radio on. She didn't know. Ever since I'd moved out of Susie and June's house, not many people did.

As I was explaining to the customer who we were, what we did, and the different types of jams we sold, the radio buzzed like an obnoxious fly.

"On this day, fifteen years ago, Isabella Prince went missing from her Beverly Hills home..."

I froze.

Of course. August eighteenth. I'd completely forgotten.

It was the first year that I hadn't remembered.

I heard a throat clear and realized the customer was giving me a concerned look. "Sorry," I told her.

"No worries." She got a jar of jam and paid. As she did, she heard the radio and made eye contact with Rebecca. "Is this the Isabella Prince case?"

Rebecca nodded.

"It's so sad. If you ask me, I think it was the parents."

Neither one of us said anything.

"Anyway, have a great day."

The customer walked away, and I gave Rebecca a look. "Can we change that, please?"

She nodded, and a moment later, we were met with the sound of 80s music.

I stood in front of the register, offering my flashiest smile at the many customers who passed.

Why couldn't people forget about me?

It had been fifteen years.

I remembered watching Daniella give some bullshit interview to the news around then, saying she'd never give up on finding my body so she could finally "have some answers."

If there was anything I knew about her, it was that she always knew how to work a camera.

It was only because of Susie that I'd made it. Susie and Balto.

As foggy as so much around that time is, that day is crystal clear.

I didn't remember how I got to the woods. Daniella must have put something in my lemonade. She and Kevin wanted me gone but didn't have the guts to make sure I was dead. They'd just left me out there and thought nature would do its work.

I was alone and cold. I'd gotten myself up to a seat when a brown-furred husky came racing towards me. He licked my face, and I laughed. A tall woman with buzzed red hair followed a moment later, calling for her dog.

Then, she saw me. "He likes you."

"Sweetheart, are you here all by yourself?" Susie had asked.

In response, I ran up to her and gave her a tight squeeze of a hug.

"What's your name?"

"Madeline," I said. I'd been into the kids' books at the time.

Susie took me to her home two hours away, near Joshua Tree, where June had dinner ready. They'd turned on a VHS of *The Princess Bride* for me to watch while I heard every other word of their conversation from the next room.

Susie had noticed the bruises on my neck and my busted lip.

I told them not to take me back under any circumstances.

When it came to what Daniella and Kevin did to me, what they'd been doing for my whole life, they adopted me as their daughter and helped me officially become Madeline.

I was ten when we moved out to Pennsylvania. June's mother had gotten sick, and we needed to be closer to her. We'd lost Balto the year before, and between that and everything else, a fresh start seemed like a great idea.

There's not much to say about the eight years that followed.

I was homeschooled, of course. I changed the color of my natural blonde hair as often as I could and always kept it cut above my shoulders.

The biggest scare happened when I was sixteen. One of the "out there" conspiracy theories about my case was that I'd run away and was living with the Amish under an assumed name. It was probably because there was a community not far from us. Once a week, they hosted a market and I'd gone to pick up some of their fresh baked bread. Someone claimed to have sighted me there.

I was on the side of the road when I caught the police's eye.

"Excuse me, young lady," one officer said.

I slowed, nearly falling off my bike.

He asked my name, asked if I knew anything about the whereabouts of Isabella Prince and then he showed me the picture. Of me, at seven years old. I shook my head. All the while, I felt like I was going to combust. "No. I don't know. Sorry."

He showed me another badly rendered picture. "She'd be sixteen now. This is what she might look like." The picture was so accurate. It got my eyes and mouth and nose right, even if my face felt a little pushed in. My hair was short and red. That was the only real difference.

Surely, I thought, he knew, especially from the way he looked at me.

Instead, he said, "Sorry for bothering you. Have a good rest of your day," and got back into his car.

I MET Henry in my last year of high school. He wasn't a boyfriend. But he was my platonic soulmate if such a thing existed. I think when I was being brought into the world, someone forgot to turn on the switch that gave me any kind of romantic desire.

It was the same year Charles Perry confessed to murdering me. It had been going on ten years since I'd disappeared, and because of it, everyone was so desperate for some kind of closure that they'd overlooked the parts of his story that didn't match up. For a while, I thought that would be the end of things.

I still didn't know how Daniella and Kevin could sit there with a straight face and pretend like they were innocent. I was tired of their faces popping up every so often, in case I'd forgotten that they existed, and seeing billboards for movies, I knew they'd produced all over town.

Henry was the one who told me about Frasier Farm. I didn't know that it was possible to live like this, away from social media and the bullshit that capitalism spews at us. We were all just happy. One with nature and the moment. And upstate New York was far enough away from everything else.

He came to take over for Rebecca after lunch. So passed a hot, lazy afternoon until just after three.

The woman's platinum blonde hair was pulled back in a tight bun, and her tortoiseshell sunglasses covered half her face. Her black denim jacket and long dress were too much for how warm it was, I thought. Her presence immediately sent a shiver down my spine, although I didn't know why at first. Not until she pushed her sunglasses up to her head.

The moment we locked eyes, I thought it was all over. Instead, Daniella shot me a perfect, pearl-white smile. "How are you today?"

"Fine."

Her gaze shot down to the jam jars.

"Let me know if you have any questions," I said automatically.

Daniella nodded, mumbling something I didn't hear.

"What was that?"

"How long have you been doing this?"

"About four years," I said. "Everything's grown fresh up the road."

Daniella nodded. "Do you ship?"

"Yeah, we can ship. Anywhere in the US, only. Not international, but maybe soon."

There was that smile again. "No worries! My husband and I love to support local. We're visiting from LA, so."

My heart felt like a beating drum. "California. Wow. I've never been there. I'd love to go someday." My lie was so effortless that I wondered why I never pursued acting like I sometimes wanted to.

Daniella shrugged. "What's your name, honey?"

"Madeline," I said.

She wrapped her hands around two jars then. One, blackberry. The other, blueberry. But she just stood there. "My daughter loved the *Madeline* books."

"Oh," I said awkwardly.

Daniella took something out of her purse. Two pictures of me. The one of me at seven. And the age-enhanced one. The latter was somehow worse than the one I'd seen six years ago. "That's Izzy. She'd be twenty-two today. We've heard rumors she lives around here, so…"

I took the picture, and as I stared into her eyes, I realized that she had no idea. "What happened to her?" I managed.

"She disappeared."

"I'm sorry to hear that," I mustered, grasping the pictures and stuffing them in my pocket.

I thought Daniella would say more. Instead, she told me she wanted to buy the two jars. My hands shook as I put them in a bag. A lump was in my throat, preventing me from speaking. She put her sunglasses back on her

head and was about to walk away. Then, she saw the clipboard we had laid out, scrawled her name, and with that,
she disappeared into the crowd.

After a moment or two, I approached the clipboard
with shaking hands. Seeing her handwriting made me feel
seven years old again.

Daniella Prince.

She'd left an email.

And a phone number.

She'd checked our "Text Me!" box.

There it was. Proof she'd been here.

Proof it wasn't my imagination.

"Are you okay?" Henry asked.

I shook my head and shoved the pictures deeper into
my pocket.

I spent the entire short drive back feeling sick to my
stomach.

What were Daniella and Kevin doing here? Were they
looking for me? Were they on vacation, and this was all a
cruel twist of fate?

I wanted answers. For now, it seemed, I'd get none.

We were pulling up to the farm by then. I threw up in
the grass as soon as we stopped and opened the car door.
Rebecca was crocheting by the well and darted right over
to help.

It was a gorgeous night. Dusk.

None of it seemed real. Rebecca put the back of her
wrist to my forehead and said I seemed like I was coming

down with something. She helped Henry clean up, and the two led me to my room to rest.

There, I promptly tore the pictures into tiny pieces.

Before dinner, Rebecca brought me a bottle of kombucha.

While everyone else ate outside, I sat alone in my room with the window cracked, wondering if this was it.

Maybe I needed to ignore it. Pretend it never happened. I'd been Madeline for longer than I'd ever been Isabella. Besides, I was an adult. No one could force me from the home I'd built here.

Whenever Daniella and Kevin talked to the news, I always wondered if there was a part of them that knew I wasn't dead. That had always kept me living in fear.

But she'd looked right at me and had no idea who I was.

That said enough.

I WOULD HAVE LEFT it alone if not for the documentary. It aired on TV about a week later when I was home in Pennsylvania with Susie and June, visiting for Susie's forty-fifth birthday. On the train, I'd gone back and forth about five hundred times about telling them. By the time June picked me up, I'd officially decided not to.

It would be another close call. My birth parents had every right to live their lives and travel wherever they pleased. That was part of why they got rid of me, wasn't it?

It was after dinner. I'd changed into my pajamas and

found my way to the couch and the TV. Susie and June were in the kitchen, cleaning up as we got ready to have cake.

The documentary must have been a few minutes in when I flipped to it.

The photograph I was met with spurred the weight of millions of memories, hitting me all at once.

Me, in a Snow White dress, in my bedroom.

I remember Daniella saying I couldn't be Snow White; my hair was long and blonde. Dad had said I could get a wig before both of them relented. I didn't need to see the pumpkin on my dresser to remember that it was Halloween.

I became a statue as I stared at that smiling girl, the one who I felt so close to yet so disconnected from. Kevin narrated. "Izzy was a perfect kid. She loved everyone and everything."

Smash cut to my parents in their living room. Holding hands, dressed professionally, putting on the waterworks for the camera.

My heart was pounding. They were asked about the many unconfirmed sightings of me in upstate New York.

"Izzy, if, somehow, you're watching this, please come home," Daniella said through crocodile tears. "We love you."

Susie came into the room shortly thereafter and saw what I was watching.

"Oh," she said.

I didn't respond.

"You know," Susie continued, "there's nothing they can do."

My hand limply wrapped around the remote as I turned it off. Right then and there would have been my chance. But I didn't say anything. I was going to handle this myself.

Henry picked me up from the train station on a perfect early morning.

"Do we still have the clipboard from the last farmer's market?" I asked once he'd gotten in the car.

"Yeah," he said. "Why?"

I inhaled. "We need to talk when you get back. It's serious."

We'd gotten breakfast sandwiches from our favorite bagel place on the way back, and sat outside and ate them by the well.

"Do you know anything about Isabella Prince?" I asked after going back and forth a million ways on how I possibly could have phrased the question.

Henry shook his head.

"Girl who went missing from Beverly Hills fifteen years ago. Her parents were two big movie producers."

"I don't think so, sorry," he said.

"Officially, she was missing, declared dead, but... Isabella Prince is me."

Henry almost dropped his breakfast sandwich. "What? You mean, your name—"

"Legally, it's Madeline, but I was born Isabella Prince.

And that woman that we saw was my mom. And it sickens me to see them... when..."

"What?"

"They tried to kill me. Before that, it was..." I winced, thinking of Daniella undressing in front of me, of Kevin coming into my bed and fondling me, and so much more. I couldn't think of how to express those things to Henry, not in words. "I'll just say that I love my life now. And I wish the first seven years had never happened."

Henry caught his breath and then looked back at me. "So, what do you want to do?"

"Call her."

"And say what?"

"I don't know. But I know I'll figure it out."

We went back into town and I got a burner phone.

That night, I went outside and I made a plan. I wasn't sure what I was expecting or how I even managed to muster up the courage, but I knew if I didn't do this, it was going to keep coming back to haunt me.

Your name is Madeline, I reminded myself. *You are twenty-two years old. You're the one in power here.*

I dialed, and then it rang.

Ring...

I looked up at the beauty that surrounded me. I heard the crickets. Moments like these, where I was one with nature, made me feel safe and peaceful.

Ring...

Maybe she wouldn't answer, and this would all be for nothing.

Ring...

"Hello?" Daniella's voice was groggy.

Fuck. This was it.

"Hello?" she repeated.

"Oh, hi," I said, putting on my cheeriest voice. "This is Madeline from Frasier Farm."

"Oh, yes," Daniella said.

I heard whispers with Kevin in the background.

"I wanted to make sure you enjoyed your visit last week."

"Very much," she said.

I inhaled. "I was the one who assisted you."

"Right."

"Madeline, like the *Madeline* books," I said.

Daniella was quiet.

I needed to cut to the chase. "Daniella, I'm so happy that you signed up to be on our mailing list." That wasn't cutting to the chase. Jeez. Fuck. Think.

"You're welcome." I could tell she wanted to shoo me off the phone.

"You know, my name wasn't always Madeline."

Breathing.

"It was Isabella."

Still nothing.

"I know Dad's there. Put it on speaker." Calling them Mom and Dad felt wrong, but I knew I needed to do it. Suddenly, a lifetime of making a concerted effort to think of them only by their given names evaporated.

More breathing.

"God, Mom, have you not figured it out?"

The phone went on speaker a moment later.

"Izzy, you're—" Mom started.

"Dead?" I scoffed. "Nice try."

"We..." Her voice was weak now.

"Didn't count on anyone finding me? Well, they did."

"What do you want from us?" Dad cut in.

"I want you to leave my name out of your mouths once and for all. You wanted me gone. So let me be gone."

"Or what?" Dad threatened.

"I'll walk into the police station, and I'll tell everyone who you are and what you did to me."

"Izzy, where are you?" Mom said. "You have to understand..."

"Understand what? I think I understand it perfectly well!" I was breathing heavily now. It was insane how easy it was for me to match their level. "What's your line, Dad? A Prince never goes back on their word?'"

I hung up the phone before either of them could respond.

Then, I cried.

I didn't hear anything about me or my case from my parents after that. Life went on as it always had.

Five years passed. I was at Frasier for another three of them. New York City had been calling me for a while by then. What made me do it was finding out my mother had died.

It was on a day very much like the one at the Farmer's Market. I had the radio on. And then, I heard the words,

"Daniella Prince, the visionary film producer, has died. She was 48." It was cancer. Aggressive. She hadn't even had a chance of beating it.

I felt lighter.

Then, the sun set that night and rose again the next morning.

Saying goodbye was hard, but it was a needed change. I was going to pursue acting. I felt free to do so. There was always the thought in the back of my mind that Dad could see me in something when he was in New York. I almost welcomed the scenario. Him, sitting feet from me, seeing the woman I'd become. I'd stare right into his eyes, and he'd know there was nothing he could do but walk away.

From my very first steps in the city, it was like someone had turned a page.

The year I was twenty-seven, it came back to me again. I'd gotten to an audition early and was having breakfast while I waited for my appointment time, taking turns between scrolling through my phone and people-watching. The latter was one of my favorite things about New York. I was always curious about people. I wondered how much of our problems in society were due to an inability or incuriosity to understand others' pain.

On my phone, I saw the article. Four words from the headline stood out. "ISABELLA PRINCE PIC GREENLIT..." They were making a movie about me. About my case. No cast or any other details yet, but it seemed legit. They quoted Dad. He'd given the project his blessing, but creatively, he would not be involved.

I set down my phone. My eyes caught a family a few booths from me. The parents didn't look anything like mine, but the girl could have been me. Blonde hair, gap-toothed smile, gingham blue dress. The waitress brought her a plate of the chocolate chip smiley face pancakes I'd seen on the menu.

I couldn't hear anything they were saying, but I watched the girl's beaming smile as the dad snapped a picture with her and the pancakes.

In that moment, everything I'd lost hit me all at once.

The Future We Were Promised

ALL I ever wanted was to be seen.

In early 2001, I was pushing twenty-six, and I'd wanted to die for over a year. In March, I had a detailed plan. I was going to fill a bathtub with hot water, get in, and slash my wrists. The only reason I hesitated was because it would be at least a week before anyone found me. By then, I was sure that my body would stink to high heaven, and I didn't want to put that on anyone.

In April, I booked *The Glass Menagerie*. I was Laura Wingfield. It was my first lead role—ever. Community theatre, sure; nothing that was going to get me out of the gift shop. But it was my first win in years.

When I called my family with the news, their reactions were muted.

"Are they paying you?" Dad asked.

"No, but it's going to be great. You guys should come see it."

"We'll have to see, Oona," Mom said. "We might be busy."

"For four weekends in a row?"

"*We'll have to see.*"

They passed me to Oliver then.

"Laura's not the lead," was my brother's response. The TV was blaring in the background, and I could hear Mom and Dad yelling at him to turn it down.

"How do you know?" I asked once I could hear myself think.

"We're reading it in school."

I hung up the phone. I knew I'd get in trouble but at that point, I couldn't have cared less.

As excited as I was to get to work, I still wasn't happy. What good were good things if you didn't have anyone to share them with?

Still, I hoped the feeling was temporary and that it would fade as soon as I got to work with the rest of the cast.

Later that week, a very interesting email appeared in my inbox.

Dear Ms. Laughlin,

My name is Maura Woodson, and I am a sophomore at Florida State University. I am reaching out because I found your name and information listed in the alumni network and was

```
impressed with all you've managed to
achieve since graduation. I was
wondering if you would be willing to
speak with me about your experiences
as an actor for a documentary
project about the performing arts at
your convenience.
```

```
I look forward to hearing from you
and possibly collaborating.
```

She was impressed with me. How? Still, I responded, and we made plans to meet at the theater before rehearsal the following night.

I got there early and hadn't been waiting for long when I saw a young woman approaching me, her posture straight. She carried a camera and tripod, and her clothes —white dress, denim jacket, dark brown hair in a low ponytail—projected confidence.

"Oona, right?" She said.

"Hi," I replied.

"Maura."

We shook hands.

"You know, you have a striking resemblance to Piper Laurie. Young Piper Laurie, though, obviously."

My face went blank. "Who?"

"Old Hollywood actress. She's been in a lot. Look her up."

I was both embarrassed and struck by how sure of herself Maura was. Sophomore in college meant she was nineteen or twenty. Whether it was because she was really going places or simply had yet to face the world, I couldn't exactly tell.

She'd barely had the chance to thank me for giving the opportunity when Cameron, the director, saw us. He turned right to Maura. "Can I help you?"

"Oona and I connected because I'm at FSU, I'm doing a project, I..."

My face flushed. I should probably have told him before we made plans. But here we were.

I was positive he was about to say something that would throw this entire plan on its head. Instead, he invited Maura in to take some footage of the rehearsal itself.

It was a small black box theater. When I was auditioning, I remembered hearing that there were sixty seats in all. "I think it's so they can brag about selling out," I told Maura as we walked in, and she started to set up her camera.

"How do you feel about the audience being right there?" Maura asked.

"I mean, you blur out the faces after a while," I replied.

Maura smiled. "You know, my best friend from home is an actress, and she says the same thing."

I was aware that Cameron's eyes were on us, even as he sorted papers for the night ahead. I pretended not to notice and turned back to Maura. "Where's home for you?"

"Minnesota," she said in an exaggerated Midwest accent.

"How do you like Florida?"

"Weather's a lot nicer here," she replied with a laugh. "Where are you from, Oona?"

"Indiana," I said.

"Family coming to see the show?"

I shook my head. "Probably not."

"Well, it's their loss."

Cameron cleared his throat and turned his attention back to Maura. "I don't mean to barge in, but this might be a good conversation to have on camera."

Maura blushed. "You're right." She lingered and got Cameron's attention again. "Hey, don't you think she looks like Piper Laurie?"

He looked at me, his gaze piercing. "Definitely."

The questions she asked me were fairly standard. It was crazy how easily I was able to lay it on thick. As I did, I saw Cameron smiling out of the corner of my eye.

"How did you get into acting?"
"When I was four years old, I'd write plays for me and my brother to perform for the rest of the family. We had a great time."

A few months earlier, Oliver confessed that he

hated acting and hated being forced to do it
with me.

What was your experience like at Florida State?
"It was great. I had an amazing education, but the
best part of it was the people I met."

If you counted the friends that broke my trust
when I found out they'd all been talking shit about
me behind my back, then sure, this was true.

What's your advice for anyone wanting to pursue a
career in the arts?
"Never give up."

I'd been an inch from throwing in the towel when
I got in this show. As exciting as it was, I knew it
wasn't going to change the trajectory of my career.

What can you tell us about this production?
"It's a Tennessee Williams classic, and this is my
dream role, so I'm excited to share it with you all."

I'd only read *The Glass Menagerie* for the first
time in the days leading up to my audition. I knew
of it but nothing more. In my defense, I hadn't
come up with the dream role line—Cameron had,
in the press release announcing we were the first

theater in Tallahassee to perform the show in forty years.

Later, after Maura got some footage of the scene where I had to let Tom back into the house after a night out, I watched her leave with a smile on her face. I'd been like that halfway through college, too. For her sake, I hoped she'd succeed and that self-doubt would never creep into her mind to the point that it overwhelmed her.

We were done by 8 p.m., but Cameron stopped me before I could leave, asking if I could talk for a second.

"Sure."

He stayed seated in the front row as I faced him. He put his papers away, and his clear blue eyes were completely and totally focused on me.

"Why didn't you tell me about your friend?" he asked.

My heart thumped as I noticed the way his button-down framed his muscular torso and tucked into his dark slacks.

He was put together, well-dressed.

I wasn't into the surfer look.

This, I was.

Stop it, I thought. *He's your director, your boss.*

"I'm sorry," I said. "It just kind of happened."

Cameron smiled. "It's not that serious. Take a breath."

"Oh..." I couldn't stop myself from blushing.

"So, what's this about your family not being able to come?" he asked.

"They've never supported anything I do," I replied.

His face tightened. "That's too bad."

I was about to take advantage of the lull in the conversation and leave when he asked if he could take me out for a drink.

WE ENDED up at a trendy bar a few blocks away from the theater, passing the clothing store where I'd worked for a month in college before I was fired for being late too many times.

I told Cameron about this story in an attempt to break the ice, and he seemed confused. "That surprises me."

"Why?"

"Because you don't strike me as someone who would slack off," he said firmly.

"I didn't care about the job," I said. "That's why."

He stopped, giving me a tired smile, his eyes fully and totally on me once again. "I can't blame you."

My eyes shot to his ring finger. I didn't see one. Maybe he had a girlfriend. Either way, while he hadn't vocalized his reasoning for taking me out, wanting to get to know me better wasn't a crime.

We were met with purple neon lights and white plush seating that felt like something straight out of an Arthur C. Clarke novel. Destiny's Child blasting from the stereo made it all the more unique and specific to this fleeting moment in time.

"I love this place," Cameron whispered in my ear.

"I've never been," I whispered back, finding myself

smiling. It was a real, genuine smile. I didn't remember the last time I'd smiled like that.

After a moment, he noticed two open seats and directed me there. "What's your poison?" he asked.

"I don't know. Surprise me."

"Sounds good." As I watched his silhouette from the counter, I thought back to the audition. There'd been a lot of girls there. I never thought I had a chance over any of them. Five, including me, were at the callback.

He's going to go with someone else, I thought. *There's no way.*

Why me?

He turned around with two sparkly blue drinks in funky glasses that looked like beakers. "This is called the Millennium, apparently," he announced, handing me one.

We clinked our glasses and drank.

"How'd you hear about this show?" he asked.

"I follow this blog that announces auditions in the area," I said. "I figured, why not?"

"I'm glad you did."

After another few sips of my drink, I worked up my courage. "So, what made me your Laura?"

"Well," Cameron said. "You understood the character."

"In what way?"

"I could tell you know what it's like…"

"What?"

"To not fit in."

I took a breath, not sure what to make of the comment.

"It's not a bad thing. I'm the same way. It's why I wanted to direct this show. I don't know if I said, but I'm teaching high school drama to a bunch of fucking obnoxious rich kids."

"How old are you?" I asked, suddenly curious.

"Forty. Does that bother you?"

"No," I said, confused. "Why would it bother me?"

"Because I'm old."

"Hey. Y2K didn't get us, right?" I said. "So, there are infinite possibilities in store."

"Cheers to that." At that point, we clinked our glasses together once more. "So, what's the five-year plan?" he asked after a beat.

"I don't know."

"You should be on Broadway. Is that what you want?"

I blushed, reminded for the first time in years of how badly I'd wanted to go to New York. "Yeah, I think so."

"You think so?"

"Well, I applied to schools out there, but I didn't get into any," I said. "And ever since I graduated, it hasn't made sense to leave."

"Tell me that you're not going to still be here when you're thirty," he said. "No, promise me."

"Okay," I whispered.

"By the way," he said. "Piper Laurie doesn't have anything on you."

My face went blank.

"She's the mom in *Carrie*," said Cameron.

"Oh," I muttered.

We both laughed.

I wasn't sure how long we were at the bar, but eventually, he drove me home. By the time I got back to my studio, I felt something. The sense that everything was going to be okay.

After showering, I lay in bed and shut off the lights, kicking my pajama shorts off and sliding my fingers to my clitoris. I imagined the feeling of Cameron's lips, his body pressed against mine. It was too easy to cum.

Afterward, as I let *la petite mort* wash through my body, I felt disgusting. Some people had loving partners to make them feel this way. I only had myself and my stupid fantasies. Freak.

In the weeks that followed, I had rehearsals to look forward to, and not only because I'd see Cameron. I was looking forward to what we were creating.

It was about a month from opening night, right after my parents told me that they for sure wouldn't be able to see the show, when it became something more.

That night, it was just me, Cameron, and Randy, the actor playing Jim. Randy was a nice enough guy, but this was the first show he'd ever been in, and he had no other experience or training to speak of when he auditioned on a whim. As much as I loved stories like his, it slowed down our piece of the show since he'd constantly ask how he should say every line.

I felt like a bitch for being upset as I was sitting on the couch and doing nothing while Randy and Cameron were discussing Jim and Laura's kiss.

"I really kiss her? We don't fake it?" Randy said.

"Yes, you really kiss her, Randy."

"Are you sure?"

As they continued back and forth, I turned away, trying to hide the red flush of embarrassment on my face. I picked up the glass unicorn—in actuality, a plastic figurine. It was such a beautiful, unique thing. I could see why Laura loved it.

They were still going, so finally, I said, "I promise I don't have bad breath."

They both looked at me in silence.

"Let's practice it, okay?" Cameron said.

The first time, his lips were tight and closed against mine. It felt more like a push than an actual kiss, and it was done a second later.

Cameron stopped us there. "No, no, no. Start over. Let it last."

Randy turned to me. "I don't want to—"

"Randy. *Kiss* her," Cameron said firmly.

We did the scene again, and it felt perfectly fine.

But according to Cameron, it wasn't enough. "Act like you like her, okay? And don't stop until I say."

Then, he stood up and took Randy's place on stage.

"Here, watch me. I'll be Jim." He looked into my eyes, and I looked into his. I gave him a slight nod as he took his hand in mine, pulled me in, and stopped short of actually kissing me.

The third time, Randy started slowly. As the pace picked up, he caressed my cheek. His tension in this kiss was gone. And something happened.

I became Laura, and I felt everything she did.

We must have been at it a few seconds when Cameron clapped his hands, signaling for us to stop. "We'll work on it. But that's time." He checked his watch. "See you both tomorrow."

Randy was already gone by the time I got my bag from the seat right next to Cameron's. I was about to wish him a good night when I felt his hand on my shoulder. I stopped my heart racing.

"Oona, you're so tense."

"What?"

In response, his hand moved to my palm. The tingle of arousal quickly spread throughout my body.

He squeezed my hand. "You have no idea how hard it is to control myself around you."

As he kissed my hand, I only had a few seconds to process what was going to happen before it actually did. I wanted this. I knew I did. He brought me into his lap and slid his hand down my pants, right onto my clit.

I moaned in pleasure. I didn't know it was possible to feel this good. Then, he leaned in and kissed me. As his lips gently stroked mine, I succumbed to the overwhelming feeling of nirvana. I'd never been kissed like *this* before.

It abruptly stopped a moment later. "Goodnight," Cameron said, breathing heavily.

There was so much I wanted to say. I opened my mouth, but he cut me off before I could say more.

"Goodnight, Oona."

I had the next day off from work, and I couldn't stop thinking about what had happened.

If I wanted it, and he wanted it, what difference did it make that he was my director?

I was single. He was single. We were both adults.

That morning, I saw an email from Maura.

```
Hey,

Hope you're doing well and that
rehearsals are going great! I wanted
to update you that a rough cut of
the doc should be done by the time
you guys close! I can't wait for you
to see it!

P.S. Can you send me ticket info when
you get a chance? I want to come!
```

Yes, I thought to myself. *Rehearsals are great. They are better than great.*

Still, I responded simply, wondering what she would think if she knew.

I was the first to arrive at rehearsals that evening. Cameron was sitting in his usual spot, center of the front row, looking over the script.

"Hi," I said with a smile as I approached.

"What is it, Oona?" he asked without looking up.

"Can we talk about last night?"

He looked up then and gave me a blank stare. "What do you mean?"

You know, I thought. *You're playing dumb, and I don't know why.* I was about to say more when Jake, the actor playing Tom, came into the theater. We both watched as he put his stuff down.

"Bathroom," Jake announced. "Be right back."

Once he left, I turned back to Cameron.

"Tonight. Stay after they leave, okay?" he said with a whisper and a smile.

So, I did.

The two hours until we were alone were agonizing.

Once we were, he took my hand. "You were less tense today."

I wanted him to touch me again. But, for now, something he'd told me the night before was playing in the back of my mind. "Do you really think I could be on Broadway?"

"Without a doubt. Is that what you want?"

I nodded.

He interlaced his fingers in mine, brought my hand to

his lips, and started to kiss it. "Is this what you want?" he asked.

"Yes," I said, pleasure bubbling up in me.

"Then we can't do it here."

"Where should we go?" I asked.

"My place won't work," he said.

"A hotel?"

"Too expensive."

"I live alone."

In any other circumstance I would have been embarrassed to bring him to my place and to my little bed. But something told me it wouldn't matter.

And it didn't.

When I woke up the next morning, he was gone, but he'd left a note.

HAD TO GET READY FOR SCHOOL. SEE YOU TONIGHT.

It lasted two weeks. Two weeks that were a blur or even a dream. Things didn't always add up, but it didn't matter. I was happy.

Cameron was always gentle. One night, he told me that he wanted to savor the moment, so I let him take pictures of me with his polaroid camera.

They were just for him, the pictures, so that when I inevitably moved on to bigger and better things in New York or LA or wherever I wanted to go, he could always remember me.

Then, with less than two weeks to go before opening night, he told me he couldn't come over. He was busy.

"When can you?" I asked.

"I don't know."

The week passed, and he was still busy.

By Monday of tech week, I approached him before the others had gotten there. "I never see you anymore."

"You see me every day," he said.

"That's not what I meant."

"I don't know what you're talking about, Oona."

Yes, you do, I thought.

He was so insistent that he hadn't that I started to wonder if I was crazy and about to realize I'd hallucinated the whole thing.

I wanted to tell someone, but who could I tell? I had no one to go to.

On Wednesday, I had work at the gift shop and was there with a girl named Ashley. I didn't know her very well, but she seemed nice enough that I didn't think she would care if I couched everything in vague details. I knew she had a boyfriend. In any case, she didn't seem like the type of person who'd ever struggled with finding love.

I had my moment to ask when the store was dead. We'd both finished cleaning and were behind the counter. "Can I ask you something?"

"Sure, what's up?"

"The guy I'm seeing hasn't called me in two weeks," I said.

"Oh. Did you make it official?"

"Well, no, but... what should I do?"

"Girl, he hasn't called you in two weeks, and he won't make it official? He's fucking someone else. Move on."

Her nonchalance caught me off guard. "Are you sure? How do you know?"

"These guys all follow the same playbook," Ashley said. "If anything, it makes them predictable."

When I said nothing, she told me she was going to the back to organize stock.

And I was left alone.

Still, I convinced myself that she was wrong. That Cameron was just busy, and he'd see me again.

I didn't get any answers until opening night when Jake and I were both doing our makeup.

"Are you fucking Cameron?" Jake asked me casually.

"What?"

"It's kind of obvious," he said.

"No," I said. "I'm not."

Jake laughed. "My real sister's a bad liar, but you're even worse," he said. "Anyway, it's not really my business, but you should know that Cameron's married. And he has two kids."

His words hit me on a delay. "He doesn't have a ring."

"Yeah, he's weird and doesn't wear one," Jake said. "Some guys are. I babysat for them like a year or two ago."

My head was spinning. "What do you mean?"

Jake's face was expressionless. "Okay. I'm probably overstepping. But I was curious because I didn't know if you knew."

Cameron walked in right then and there, and I couldn't meet his gaze.

That night, I noticed Maura in the front row.

Afterwards, I had to pretend like nothing was wrong, like everything was perfectly fine. I'd done something very wrong, and I couldn't help but feel guilty for it even though I didn't know.

He'd never said anything about his wife. His kids. He didn't even wear a ring. How was I supposed to know?

While we were all mingling after the show, Maura approached me with a huge smile on her face. "Oh my gosh, you were fantastic! Congratulations!"

"Thanks," I said. I'd spotted Cameron out of the corner of my eye, talking to an audience member. He had his arm on a woman's back. His wife's. She was beautiful, with long dark hair.

"Soon, I'll have a cut for you," Maura said. "Bear with me. It'll be my gift. Your memento of the moment."

"Yeah." I felt sick. As I looked back at Cameron and his wife, I realized there was nothing I could do but forget. And pretend it had never happened.

For the rest of the run, pretending drove me crazy. Everything about the show was ruined. It ended with a whimper. I was worse off than I'd been before, and my only crime was in believing that someone could see me. Want to be with me.

Maura was having a premiere of her film on campus around then, and I made up an excuse not to go. She told me not to worry and let her know if I wanted a VHS.

A few days after closing, I was walking home from work when I saw a familiar woman with dark hair approach me.

I stopped.

"Oona," she said. Her face was stern as she crossed her arms.

No. This wasn't...

"You're so young," she said. "I almost feel bad for you."

"You're..."

"Lori. Cameron's wife."

Fuck. "I didn't know. I swear to God. I didn't know."

She continued to stare me down, and I couldn't tell if she believed me. Suddenly, the anger vanished, replaced with sadness. "God, how old are you?"

"Twenty-five."

"You don't look a day over eighteen," Lori said, almost inaudibly. She sighed. "I was going to send those pictures of you to the news. Ruin your life. Ruin his. But..."

I froze.

"I don't think I will. I've got a family to look after. I wanted to say that I forgive you."

Back in my apartment, I cried until my pillow was soaked.

That summer, I was at my most isolated. I didn't go out for any auditions. The thought of doing so, even if I knew he'd have no part of it, made me clam up. I don't know how I even managed to eat and shower.

It took until the first week of September before I had the courage to email Maura.

```
Hey, sorry I've been out of contact.
Crazy busy couple of months. I'd
love a VHS if you still have one.
```

```
Oona
```

On the 11th, I was scheduled to work a full day at the gift shop. The phone rang that morning when I was still in bed.

"This goes without saying, but we're closed today. Stay home, stay safe," my boss told me.

"What are you talking about?"

"Good God, Oona, turn on your TV."

On September 14th, I heard back from Maura.

```
Hey!!!! I hope you're okay and
taking care of yourself. I was
really shaken by this past week (I
still am) and I haven't been on
email. I've got a tape with your
name on it. If you're close, maybe I
could drop it by? xx
```

It took a moment before I wrote back.

```
That sounds great.
```

Yesterday Once More

MASHA PULLS UP to the lake and a beautiful summer sunset as she tries to remember her many happy memories here.

As a child, first with Mom, Dad, and Alex. The four of them, together, without a care in the world.

The next was in high school, right after Owen got his driver's license. She could still remember the taste of vanilla ice cream on his lips.

She won't do it here. There are too many people. She'll have to go further into the woods, on the trail.

After parking and getting out of her car, she stops and takes a breath, smelling the lake water, the trees, the dirt, the sand. She sees the orange and pink in the sky and thinks it seems very much like a painting.

She takes one last look at her car. She and the '07 Malibu have been through a lot. Now, she leaves with a carefully placed note on the dashboard, folded to look like a parking pass from far away.

Masha looks down at her dress. The red floral one. She'd felt pretty in it once, but now she can't bring herself to feel much of anything—except the weight of her purse and the gun that sits at the bottom of it. Somehow, she finds her way to a bench and sits.

It's a warm, perfect night.

She sees the ice cream stand and thinks about getting some. But she stays put. The line is too long, and she can't bear the thought of standing.

I'm so tired of it all, she thinks.

She'd been a happy kid, popular at school, and destined for a vibrant ballet career. If she closed her eyes hard enough, she could hear the *Swan Lake* theme, feel a thousand eyes on her, and remember what it was like to be on top of the world. It would always fade to screeching tires, crashing metal, the beep of hospital machines, and words that still rung in her ear. "You have to focus on getting well."

She found Sawyer in the weeks she was still recovering at home. He was down in Illinois but could coach her virtually. This man's life had been forever changed in a car accident, too, one that had killed his family. If he could rebuild, Masha knew she could too.

She'd truly thought there'd be a silver lining to this chapter in her life.

Yet, she couldn't remember much of what they'd talked about, only that Alex didn't like Sawyer.

"You're spending all your savings on this dude?" Alex would say. "Masha, you should be moving out of Mom and Dad's, getting another job—"

"I don't want another job! I want to dance! And he's the only one that understands."

On and on it went.

Sawyer told her that the problem was her mindset, that she could have anything she wanted in life, and that the fact that she hadn't meant she was letting her blockages get in the way.

There would be glimmers of hope, and then it would all get snatched away. From Cody cheating on her to the teaching position not working out and her car breaking down when she'd been ready to pay off her student loans.

Three years on, the car crash seemed more and more like one of those bad things that happened for no other reason other than life wasn't fair.

Masha isn't sure how long she's been sitting when she hears someone calling her name. He had to say it a few times for her to realize.

Owen. He looks the same, prep school style and all. The only difference is that his jawline is a little more defined. "Oh my God, it's really you."

Masha swallows, carefully adjusting her purse. "It's really me."

"What are you doing here?" he asks, sitting next to her.

"Just..."

He doesn't give her the chance to say more. He's eying

the long scar on the side of her face, a physical reminder of the day everything went wrong. "I heard about what happened. I donated to the GoFundMe. Are you okay? Is everything okay?"

"Yeah," Masha says without meeting his gaze.

He tries to sit next to her. Startled, Masha shifts, and the gun and shell casings fall out of her bag and onto the grass.

This is it, Masha thinks. *He'll ask, and I won't have the guts to do it anymore.*

Owen stares and laughs. "Oh my God." He picks up the shell casings and hands them to her. "You're not about to commit a mass shooting, are you?"

The last is supposed to be a joke. Alex would be offended by something like this, and it's probably not okay to say, but Masha can't bring herself to care. "No, I'm... uh. I don't feel safe." Her face is red hot as the lie comes out.

Owen takes it at face value. "Hey, no worries. As long as you don't shoot me."

Masha nods, shaking as she puts the gun back into her purse.

He walks away. She watches as he joins a group of friends. Maybe he'll stop, bring them over, and introduce her. They'll drink a few beers, and she'll have a decent time. Maybe even laugh. By then, she'll have forgotten about why she came.

But he doesn't. Of course, he doesn't. Why would he?

In the middle of this busy, vibrant place, she couldn't feel more alone.

The last conversation with Sawyer rings through her head.

"Masha, if you're not serious about getting better, I can't ask you to keep wasting my time," he said.

"I am serious."

"Then why have we made no progress? It's been three years. I don't understand you."

She'd had nothing to say.

"It's up to you whether you want to get better, okay?"

"But they diagnosed me with depression and borderline—"

"Those diagnoses are all bullshit, you know? To keep you down and to keep the pharmaceutical industry's pockets lined. If you can't make an effort to get better, then I can't keep you on."

That night, Masha saw her whole life pass before her. It was one filled with false starts and false hopes.

The next day, she bought a gun.

She holds on, trying to feel the sun on her skin, for any spark of hope. As if in answer, the sky clouds over, and the sun disappears.

And she walks into the woods.

In the end, she thinks of Owen, of senior prom. Of baking apple pie on Thanksgiving. Picking lilacs from her yard in spring. Her first day of ballet classes. And *Swan Lake*, and the moment she got the call.

"Will you be our Swan Princess?"

There are so many memories. But those days are gone. Better to leave them untainted.

It's too late.

In case anyone still cares,

By the time you read this, I'll be dead. You'll find my body in the woods somewhere. I'm sorry for not saying more, but there's nothing any of you could have done.

I used to have so much hope for the way my life was going to go. I thought it was going to be like a Disney fairytale. And even when I got a little older and realized that's not real life, I still believed in the goodness of the world. But I've since come to the conclusion that it doesn't matter what some people do. They're just never enough.

Sawyer, thank you for trying to help me. You did your best. I'm sorry I let you down.

Mom, Dad, Alex, find comfort in the good times.

These past few weeks, I kept waiting for someone to notice that I'm barely alive as is. If this was a movie, this would be the part where someone reminds me why I'm worth it.

I'm going to stop pretending that everything works out for the best. Whatever lies past this life is going to be better anyway.

Thank you, and again, I'm sorry.

Masha

This Time Tomorrow

I WAS two weeks from turning twenty-eight when I met Wendy and Sawyer. I had no idea how they'd even managed to notice me. I didn't think anyone did. At work, I kept my head down, crunching numbers in a spreadsheet from 9 a.m. to 5 p.m. every Monday through Friday. I went home each night to my shoebox room in an apartment with roommates I barely saw. My weekends were spent doing laundry and running errands. I didn't talk to anyone, and that was the point. It was never worth it. I hadn't always thought like that, but life had a way of wearing me down.

I kept seeing a life I hadn't experienced pass me by. In my early twenties, I was met with the common refrain of "Don't worry, you're young. You have time. Everything's going to work itself out." I watched the people I grew up with go through all of the life milestones—dates, marriages, kids, a social life, some sense of purpose—while

I stayed stuck. It only got worse the more time that passed, not better. There was nothing I could do to stop it, only to watch my life slip away from me the closer I got to thirty.

Every morning, from the moment I opened my eyes, all I wanted to do was go back to sleep, stay in bed, and do anything I could to forget about my worthless, pathetic existence. It had been like this for the past year and a half and it seemed like it would be like this for the foreseeable future. The monotony had gotten so unbearable that the only thing keeping me from taking a knife to my wrists was the absurd notion that it wasn't going to be like this forever.

It was the first week of November when I found myself at the local coffee shop. I'd gotten up early to finish my errands, so I could have the rest of the day to make progress on my novel.

I was sitting by the window, staring at a blank document, watching the multicolored leaves fall onto the ground. There was one particular one that caught my eye, the sole golden yellow leaf in a sea of orange and red, begging to be noticed. I wondered if its unique nature was both a blessing and a curse. The sun made the leaf almost glow. It was beautiful. But maybe it didn't want to stand out. Maybe it was tired of being different. Unique. Extraordinary.

I took a sip of my caramel apple latte—sweet, autumnal heaven—as I gazed at the outside scene, something straight out of an Edward Hopper painting. My eyes drifted away and back to my blank document. Usually, coming to the coffee shop helped me think. But that afternoon, I couldn't find the inspiration.

I clicked out of the document, opened Facebook, and found myself searching for Julian's page. We hadn't been friends in forever, but I still could see his profile picture. It was a selfie taken in his car, the sunlight reflecting off his blond hair and beard. After nine years, I'd found myself trying to remember him—the sensation of his lips on mine, how he felt on top of me, and how he always knew what to do to get me to orgasm. But more than the sex itself was after. He'd look at me with this feeling like he couldn't believe I was real, tuck a strand of hair behind my ear, tell me I was beautiful, and we'd lay there for a while. They were all signals to my brain, telling me *you're not alone. You're loved. You have a place in the world.* I'd feel it when we walked hand-in-hand around campus and he smiled at me as he rubbed his thumb down my palm.

Even looking at his picture was enough to make my desire ache. I knew I was just holding onto a memory of the way he used to make me feel, not wanting to be with him again. It was almost easier to be alone when I was still a virgin, and I didn't know what I was missing.

It had been so long since anyone had touched me. I was so lonely it made my body hurt.

I closed out the tab, sighed, and looked back out the window, trying to find some sort of comfort in the scene. I tried to look for the yellow leaf, but it was gone, buried by the other ones.

"It's Ingrid, right?" a woman's voice called.

It took me a moment to realize that someone was standing next to me. I turned and saw her dark, chin-length bob and dimpled smile. I recognized her from work. We'd pass by each other in the halls and in the break room. There was also the one time when she'd caught me letting out a much-needed cry in the bathroom, but her name escaped me.

Next, she spoke. "I'm Wendy, I'm HR at Browning. You're—"

"Bookkeeping," I said with a dry smile, half-closing my laptop.

"Is that a new story?" she asked.

I froze. I'd never talked to anyone about my writing. "Yeah," I said. I was about to ask how she knew when she answered my question.

"I read the short you published. The one about the small town and the bomb threats. It was really good."

My face flushed. "You read that?"

"Yeah, my boyfriend's a writer too, so he has a subscription to—"

"*Starlight*?" I'd found Starlight Magazine on a list of "20 Paying Magazines To Submit Your Writing To" and applied to every one. They were the only ones who accepted me. The prize? $25 and a free copy of the magazine. It was exciting but not exactly life-changing, and hard to imagine it was something someone would actually notice me for.

She nodded. "Is it based on a true story?"

"Nope," I said. "Fiction."

Wendy looked at me with awe. "What's your new one about? The one you're writing." I blushed, and she added, "If you can tell me."

"Sure. It's about an Olympic sprinter, and she gets caught using steroids."

"Wow, and what inspired it?" Wendy asked.

"Um, I guess I'm interested in the idea of second chances."

"That's so cool, Ingrid," Wendy said. "I don't know how you do it. Sorry for asking you so many questions, by the way. I'm a big reader. I always have been. Maybe one day I'll get to brag about how I used to work with you."

I nodded and started to open my laptop again as Wendy took two steps toward the register. I thought I was in the clear when she caught my attention again.

"Hey, I'd love to have you meet my boyfriend some-time," she said. "I feel like you and he would get along."

"Sure," I said quietly, hoping she wasn't actually serious.

Wendy sensed the conversation was over and told me she'd see me at work.

I did the same and turned back to my laptop.

I RAN into her on Monday in the break room at lunch. That day was cold and windy, and there wasn't a ray of sun in the sky. It was the type of weather that could really do a number on your mood. I'd been taking slow bites of my peanut butter and jelly sandwich. The bread was dry, and I'd way overdone it on the jelly. The chips I'd packed were broken and stale, too.

She'd come in then, taking a bottled smoothie out of the refrigerator. She was on the phone when she waved in my direction. Her conversation, seemingly to her boyfriend, went in one ear and out the other. After a moment, she hung up, still holding the smoothie in her hands.

"Hey," she called to me. "How's it going?"

"It's Monday," I said.

She looked at my meal. "How's the PB&J?"

"Fine," I whispered.

Wendy raised her eyebrows. "Do you want a real meal? Because Sawyer—sorry, that's my boyfriend—and I are going to lunch, and you're welcome to come."

I looked at my sandwich and then back at her. Something—call it a gut feeling—compelled me to say yes.

She and I rode to the Italian restaurant on Main Street in her Lexus. Part of me wondered why she was working at the same place as me when she could afford luxury cars and lunches out because I doubted Browning paid her that much.

"By the way," Wendy said, "it's on us."

I opened my mouth to protest but stopped short. The second we stepped in, and I caught a whiff of the upscale atmosphere, I knew I'd never be able to afford it on my own. The green shag carpet, white tablecloths, and sepia-toned photos of Hollywood stars may have screamed stuck in the eighties, but still, it was a vibe.

Wendy must have seen my expression and added, "We are *honored* to pay for the meal of an author that's been published in *Starlight*."

I blushed and said nothing, as she'd already made eye contact with the man, who must have been Sawyer. I looked at him. He was handsome and square-jawed and seemed like he belonged more on Wall Street than in Joliet, Illinois. I saw the wrinkles around his eyes and streaks of gray in his neatly cut dark hair, and then back at Wendy. There had to have been at least twenty years between them. Interesting.

The two waved, and Wendy motioned for me to follow. As they exchanged a quick kiss, I avoided their gaze and instead looked down at my menu.

My eyes drifted to the pastas and a dish that made my stomach growl just reading the description. Spicy garlic sauce. Parmesan cheese. Jalapeño. Spinach. Chicken Sausage. I looked at the price—$35 for a plate—and balked.

Sawyer caught my attention then, speaking in a commanding tone. "See anything that looks good?" I opened my mouth and was about to speak when he said, "Order whatever you want. Seriously."

I pursed my lips and noticed his watch. Rolex. I gulped.

The waiter came. I wasn't going to order a drink, but they both did, so I did, too. I got a pinot noir, not realizing there were multiple on the menu. I pretended to know what he was talking about when he brought up dryness and flavor profiles and picked one with some bougie French name on the sole basis that it was French.

After the waiter left, I turned to Wendy. "What's Pidge going to say when we go back to work day drunk?" Marcus Pidgeon was the big cheese of Browning, but everyone called him Pidge, a nickname he hated. He took himself way too seriously. As much as he reminded me of the Businessman from *The Little Prince*, I didn't like jumping in whenever the other employees whispered behind his back. I knew he had a life and a family he went home to. Less than an hour in Wendy's presence was changing all of that.

"He won't even know," Wendy said, a smile curling onto her face.

Sawyer watched us with a grin, then turned to me. His gaze was piercing. He saw right through my skin to the fibers of my bones. I could have no secrets with him. "How long have you been a writer?"

"My whole life."

"And have you published anything else?"

I shook my head.

"Well, I hope this is only the start. Your..." He trailed off, then found his words with a snap of his fingers. "Your story is such a beautiful exploration of trauma and how it seeps through generations."

"Thanks," I said quietly.

"I hope they paid you handsomely for it," he said.

I snorted, and he looked at me quizzically. I had a moment before I realized he wasn't going to let this go. I thought about what to say and about how to phrase it. I was at the point where getting paid a living wage for my work felt like a far-off pipe dream. Nothing else in my life had gone right. Getting published in the magazine was a breadcrumb. I'd had many of them in my life. Escaping the Midwest for college was one. Meeting Julian was another. But they were all breadcrumbs leading to nowhere. My gaze caught Sawyer's Rolex, and suddenly I was lost for how to vocalize any of that. "Take a wild guess."

"A thousand?"

This sent me into an uncontrollable fit of laughter. "Try twenty-five."

"Twenty-five hundred?"

"No. Twenty-five dollars."

"That's a damn shame, Ingrid."

He's got to be buttering me up, I thought, still unable to stop my laughter. But why? Either that or they were encouraging me because they thought it was the polite thing to do. As the waiter returned with our drinks and we ordered lunch, Wendy stared at me with the same intensity.

"You have a gift," Sawyer said.

"Thank you," I whispered. When neither spoke, I added in a rush, "It's the dream to be a writer full-time."

"What?" Sawyer said with a sarcastic grin. "You don't want to be stuck at Browning your whole life?"

"No," I replied. I felt my cheeks redden, and there wasn't anything I could do to stop it. In front of Wendy, it was embarrassing. But it wasn't about being attracted to him. Instead, it was about something deeper: being seen.

Sawyer looked straight into my eyes. "Ingrid, I want to invite you to my lake house this weekend."

I froze. "What do you mean?"

"I mean that, every weekend, I host a group of like-minded people. We talk about the world. We connect. We have drinks. We have real conversations. We live in the moment."

I just stared at him.

"Call it a respite from the day to day," he said with a grin.

I paused. So much was floating through my head. *Who are you? Where did you come from?* "Yeah, um—"

"Oh my God, Ingrid, you'd love it. It's up in Lake Forest," Wendy said, cutting me off.

My cheeks flushed. For a flash, I wondered why they were both acting like we were all the best of friends when she and I had never exchanged words until two days before. "So, Sawyer," I said with a gulp, "you're a writer too?" My cheeks got even more red. I hadn't meant to dodge the invite so bluntly, but it took me so off guard. As I waited for his reply, I hoped they didn't think it was an outright refusal.

"Mostly non-fiction. I'm very interested in helping others take control of their lives by encouraging them to think outside of the box."

I nodded, quietly absorbing his words.

"If you have anything else you think is ready, I'd love to take a look and see if I can help you out."

"Uh, yeah," I stammered. "Not now, but I'll let you know."

He turned to Wendy. "You two will stay in touch."

She beamed a smile at me, and I managed a nervous one in return.

The food came. We'd talked mostly about politics, the state of the world, and how no one ever stopped to pay attention to the things that matter. Before I could blink, an hour had passed, Sawyer paid the bill and we all walked outside together. The wind had picked up, and I could barely feel my face. He'd kissed her goodbye before heading to his car, and I followed Wendy to hers. It was quiet as we began the drive, a fleeting respite from the afternoon of work awaiting us underneath the office's harsh fluorescent lighting.

I felt a pain in my shoulders then and tried to roll them back. I knew I had a bad habit of slouching. My gaze caught my reflection in the windows. I could have been beautiful in another life, maybe, if I had skin that wasn't covered in protruding veins, stretch marks, and acne. Maybe in that life, I had the energy to put on makeup in the morning, my hair was a less nondescript shade of brown, and I could brush it without static flying in every direction.

"You all right?" Wendy asked when we were stuck at a light.

I must have been zoned out because it took me a second to respond to her. "Yeah. Sorry. Just tired."

She gave me a pitied look that I recognized all too well. People had been giving it to me my whole life. I got it so often I could almost hear their thoughts. *Poor, pathetic, Ingrid, not a second further in life at 27 then she was at 21.*

"Thank you for lunch," I said. "It was nice."

Wendy smiled.

"How did you and Sawyer meet? Just curious."

"Well, camping last summer, if you can believe it," she said. "I do a solo trek up to Kettle Moraine every year, and we got to talking and, yeah."

"So, if he's loaded, why the heck are you still at indentured servit—I'm sorry, Browning?"

"Oh, well," she replied with a blush. "I help him. You should really come to his lake house. He brews his own beer and sells it in little farmers' markets in town. And there's this girl, Leilani, and her brother, Kai. They make soap and candles. Everyone's artistic and supportive. Really great people. If you're not busy, of course. Like, everyone's got jobs and lives, and it's just a break."

"I'll have to see," I said, knowing full well I had nothing going on.

"And," she rushed out, "you should really show Sawyer your work. He'll want to help you. Like, he's had books published and stuff."

I nodded, wondering, for a moment, why publishing one story in one magazine was so impressive to him if he was a big-time author. "So, does he write full-time?"

Wendy shook her head. "No, not exactly. He does a lot of different things." She smiled at me again.

I thought it over in my head. Between a weekend of listening to pretending I couldn't hear Jenna and her boyfriend having sex in the next room, Sara hogging the kitchen and blasting the worst music to ever exist, and an escape from all of that, I knew what I was going to do.

That night, I wanted to look up Sawyer's books, but I realized I'd never even known his last name. So I had to find Wendy at lunch the next day and ask her.

She beamed as she told me. It was a slow day, and I was ahead of work, so I made sure Pidge wasn't around and googled

He'd published one book of his own and had contributed to an anthology. The former was called *Be Your Authentic Self.*

"In the noise of today's world, how do you live truly and authentically?" The blurb asked. "A graduate of Harvard and 20-year veteran of Wall Street, Sawyer Hancock's perspective on life was forever changed when he tragically lost his wife and two young children in a car accident. After a year of traveling the world, he's returned with all he knows and shares easy, actionable steps to overcoming grief, cutting through the noise of everyday life, and prioritizing what truly matters."

I downloaded the audiobook, narrated by Sawyer

himself, popped my headphones in, and went back to work.

Sawyer's voice provided the background for his life; growing up poor, working from the time he was fifteen. By eighteen, he was an orphan, having lost his mother to cancer and his father to suicide within a year. As I listened, everything focused around his words, and before I knew it, forty minutes had passed.

Time had never gone so fast before.

By the end of the day, I'd blown through three hours, only stopping because I was working on something that needed a little more focus.

I caught Wendy as we were both leaving, realizing I'd never officially told her I was in for the weekend. So, I did.

"Oh, that's great. We're so looking forward to it."

"Hey, I've listened to a good chunk of his book," I said. "I didn't realize he'd been through so much."

She beamed. "He has, and he still believes the world is a good place."

For the rest of the week, I'd listen to Sawyer's book whenever I could. About halfway in, he wrote about the nature of the afterlife. His thesis was that our bodies were only vehicles for our souls. There was no reason to be afraid of death because we'd be onto something better, something that we couldn't even conceptualize here on earth. I didn't know if I believed it, but it was enticing. The only reason I hadn't tried to kill myself, as much as I often wanted to, was that nonexistence always terrified me more than sticking it out. I'd experienced true happiness before. I had to think that more of those days were in store.

In the evenings, I revised my first chapter so that it was in a good enough place to show him. In between it all, I kept an eye on the weather so I could know what to pack. It was the time of year when it could vary wildly from one day to the next. It was going to be sunny all weekend. Mid 50s. That had to be a good sign.

By Thursday, I'd finished his book. That afternoon, Wendy found me at my desk. "I was thinking I could pick you up in the morning, and we could leave straight from here tomorrow," she said.

"Sounds perfect," I replied.

She smiled at me. "We are really looking forward to having you."

THE NEXT MORNING, Wendy was outside my apartment building at 8:30 on the dot and with two coffees sitting in the drink cups. I didn't quite know how to respond as I saw they were from the café where we'd run into each other the previous weekend.

After I put my bag in the trunk and got in the passenger seat, she handed me one. It was a caramel apple latte.

"Happy early birthday," she said. "I saw on your file that it's next week. I'm not a stalker."

"Thank you so much," I said.

"I didn't know what you liked but I noticed you were drinking one the other day, so."

"Thank you," I repeated, my face turning red.

"I'm sorry, I hope I'm not overstepping," Wendy said.

"No, it's just..." For a moment, I lost my train of thought, unsure if I wanted to share what was on my mind.

"What?"

"I'm not used to people doing nice things for me."

There was that pitying look from Wendy again. "I'm sorry."

"It's okay. Thank you for the coffee."

She turned her attention to the road and started to drive. The morning air was crisp and perfect and Wendy had the windows cracked. I took a drink and closed my eyes, letting the hot, sweet liquid dissolve on my tongue as I inhaled the scent of autumn.

For a moment, however brief, I felt like I could be somebody.

Work itself didn't matter. What did matter was, around the later afternoon, when I went to the bathroom only to hear Wendy's voice coming from the stall next to mine.

"We definitely did. You just don't remember."

A pause.

Her voice raised. "You were busy! And it is *my* car!"

Another pause as a man's voice, his words incoherent, came from the other end.

"I can't read your mind!" she yelled. "Communication's a two-way street!"

We exited our stalls at the same time. I saw Wendy, palms pressed heavily onto the side of the sink as she tried to catch her breath. She saw me and gave me a wry look.

"Everything okay?"

She nodded, blinking back tears. "Yeah... it's just... anyway, it doesn't matter."

I gave her a nod and washed my hands.

"You'll be ready by five?" Wendy asked.

"Yeah," I managed, leaving the bathroom shortly thereafter. I hoped everything was okay, but it wasn't like I was the person to go to for relationship advice.

By 4:42, I was staring at the clock, watching with agony as the minutes inched by. *This will be a story you tell someday,* I thought.

I suddenly remembered that I needed to print my chapter, as there was no internet at the lake house. I opened my personal drive and put in the request. I had just approached the printer and noticed when I caught eyes with Pidge, collecting my pages.

We exchanged an awkward glance.

"Happy Friday," he said.

"Happy Friday."

"Is this what you really do every day?" he asked curtly.

"No. I—"

"We've all got to have hobbies." He shoved the chapter in my hands. "But keep them outside of work."

"Understood." I turned my back and walked to my desk so he wouldn't see me roll my eyes. I felt tension creeping into my neck and shoulders.

Not much longer now.

WITH TRAFFIC, the drive would take almost two hours. At least it was a gorgeous autumn day. It was so quiet for the first portion of the drive that I felt unnerved. There was a distant, glazed look in Wendy's eye.

"Are you sure everything's alright?" I asked.

She kept her eyes on the road. "Huh?"

"You were fighting with Sawyer earlier, weren't you? In the bathroom?"

"Oh," she said. "That. Yeah... It's fine."

"I'm sorry," I managed.

Wendy shrugged. We drove for a little longer in silence before she turned to me once again. "By the way, did you tell anyone you were coming with us?"

"No," I said, confused as to what it mattered.

"Got it." It was another few minutes before she pulled up Spotify and handed me her phone. "Put on whatever you like."

The comment triggered a memory I didn't know I still had. Julian's voice in my ear, saying, "You know music after 1975 exists, right?" He'd passed it off as a joke, but I knew it had been a genuine dig at my tastes. My thumb hovered over the search bar and back at Wendy. *Fuck it.* I searched for "Space Oddity."

A smile spread across her face from the song's first notes. "David Bowie?"

I nodded, blushing. "He's one of my favorites."

"I knew you were cool," she said. She started to sing along, and just like that, the tone shifted.

I<small>T WAS</small> dark by the time we pulled up to the house. The wide glass windows and angled corners were straight out of the midcentury. I'd think we'd have gone back in time.

There were two other cars there: a sleek black Maserati and a blue Prius covered in all kinds of bumper stickers. One, "If you can read this, you're too close," made me laugh.

As we parked and took a moment to collect ourselves, I looked at my phone and noticed I was completely out of bars.

Wendy gave me a look.

"No service," I explained.

"Yeah. I don't get it up here either. It's nice to have a break."

I sighed and put my phone in my bag. It wasn't like anyone was going to call me anyway.

As we stepped out of the car, we heard voices and the glow of a crackling fire. Things had cooled down since earlier in the day, but still, it was a beautiful night. "They're this way," she said. "We'll get our bags later."

The voices got louder, and the scent of woodsmoke more intense as we rounded a cobblestone path.

Sawyer was leaning in and talking to a woman with long, wavy black hair and light brown skin who appeared to be my age. A man who resembled her was sitting close, too, though more focused on his beer and the hum of the night. My gaze was immediately locked on the lake, so quiet and still.

"Ingrid," Sawyer's voice boomed.

I turned. Wendy was beside me still, but I noticed his gaze was entirely on me. She tried to break the awkwardness by leaning in and kissing him. He obliged for a moment before grabbing a beer out of the outdoor mini fridge. The others were looking at me too.

"Won't you sit?" He leaned in and whispered in Wendy's ear. "Get Ingrid a beer, please."

She turned back to the mini fridge and got one for me. "This is Sawyer's brew. It's a special fall blend, right, honey?"

He nodded. I took the beer from her and took my seat, letting myself be warmed and comforted by the glow of the fire.

The unknown pair introduced themselves. "Leilani," said the woman with a smile and a wave.

"Kai," the man echoed, shaking my hand.

"Where do you guys live?"

"Kenosha," said Kai.

"We're from Honolulu originally," Leilani added.

"Why come here?" I asked with a wry laugh.

"Dad moved for work when we were sixteen," Kai

explained. He gestured to Leilani. "We're twins. We have a little home goods store. We just opened..."

"Six months ago," Leilani said with a glowing smile.

"Awesome," I replied. My gaze shifted back to Sawyer and Wendy. He had his arm tight around her as he slipped something in her hand. It was a bottle opener, which she then gave to me.

"Slow down," he said to her. "Think about what you're doing before you do it."

"It's not a problem," I said, his sharp tone making me uncomfortable.

Sawyer ignored me and addressed the rest of the group. "Well, because Wendy decided she needed new tires for her car, unfortunately, we will have to eat in tonight."

"No worries," said Leilani.

I opened the bottle and took a sip. It was, indeed, delicious.

He gestured to me. "Ingrid's a writer. A very good one."

Leilani turned to me with a beaming smile. "What have you written?"

"Short stories, mostly, but I've got a novel in the works," I said. "And I don't know about very good, but I think I'm all right."

Sawyer smiled at me. "She's great." He turned to Wendy again. "Why don't you get dinner started?" He turned to Kai and Leilani. "Help her with whatever she needs." Then, to me. "I'll look at your pages if you want."

"Sure... I... they're in my backpack, in the car."

His gaze moved back to Wendy, and he gave her a look that she seemed to understand.

It was completely dark by the time she'd returned with my bag and had taken the other stuff into the house, Kai and Leilani trailing behind her.

Once they all were gone, he and I had a moment alone. He gave me his full focus, his eyes staring right through me, just like he'd done at the restaurant.

"I know all of them already, but I want to get to know you," he said.

"All right, well... Is everything okay between you and Wendy?"

"Just fine," he said dryly.

After a moment, I fished the printed pages out of my bag. Sawyer turned on some kind of light so he could see. He sat there and read, and I awkwardly sipped my beer. After some indistinguishable amount of time, he put the pages aside and leaned in closer to me.

"You have a gift," he said.

I blushed. "Thanks."

"Look, I mean it. I know you didn't believe me when I told you at the restaurant, but you really do."

I said nothing.

"The way the world's treated you isn't fair."

I pursed my lips.

"Ingrid, do you have a boyfriend?"

My face flushed. "No." *Don't make me talk about Julian. I don't want to talk about Julian.*

"But you did?"

"Yes."

"Why did it end?"

"He thought I was too clingy and that I lacked self-esteem," I muttered.

"How long has it been?"

"Nine years," I rushed out.

"You haven't been together for nine years? And you still love him?"

"Well," I said. "I don't know about love, but he's the only one that made me come close to feeling that way."

"And there's been no one else in nine years?" He asked, his voice tinged with disbelief.

I shook my head. "No, I... I suppose I'm still looking... for so many things."

He gave me an empathetic nod. "When I read your writing, I can tell that you've been hurt," he said. "It's not an easy thing to be vulnerable."

"It comes naturally to me, I guess," I said, barely audibly.

He smiled at me, and I noticed for the first time that his teeth were perfect: white, straight, right out of a dental magazine. "You're going to inspire so many people with your words someday."

I pursed my lips.

"Why do you look at me like that?" Sawyer asked.

"Sorry, it's just... people told me those things my whole life. Well, when I was in high school and into college. They don't so much anymore."

"They think because you're twenty-eight, your life is set?"

I didn't bother to correct him on my age. "Something like that."

His gaze remained on mine, and something about its intensity compelled me to speak.

"Every time I think I've had enough, I see something that inspires me to keep going. A little flash of... something beautiful, here or there. A gold leaf in a sea of red and yellow ones. That first sip of coffee... the memory of what it was like to be loved by another person... being out here... far away from it all."

Sawyer smiled at me again, and I realized I was done with my beer. "Do you want another one?"

I nodded, and he got out two, one for him, one for me. We sat and drank. "I read your book," I said. "Well, listened to it."

"I hope you got something out of it."

"I did." Something had been gnawing at me ever since I'd read it, so I took the lull in the conversation as an opportunity to ask. "Do you really believe that when we die, it's not the end?"

"You don't?"

"I don't know," I answered. "It'd be nice, I guess... but I think I believe we can only ever live in the moment because nothing else is guaranteed."

Sawyer was about to bring his beer to his lips then, but he stopped. The look he gave me was so intense that I thought I'd done something wrong. Instead, he just nodded.

THE NIGHT WAS a blur until some time later. We had dinner —pasta with homemade pesto sauce and chicken, some of the best I'd ever tasted, and red wine, top shelf. Leilani showed me to my room. It was a king bed with a lush red and gold comforter and decorative throw pillows that reminded me of what one might see in a Disney fairytale. I knew from just one look that I was going to get the best sleep of my life.

After I showered and changed clothes, I found my way back downstairs. I felt a rush of cold air first and then smelled the scent of weed. I saw Kai sitting out on the patio and went to join him.

"Hey," I said. "Where's your sister?"

"Resting. Want a light?"

I nodded. Between the beer, the wine, and now this, I was probably going to regret things in the morning, but it didn't matter. Come Sunday afternoon, I'd be back home, and then on Monday, back to work, and I knew it wouldn't take long for the bad feelings to come rushing back. The drugs were numbing me to all of that. The longer it stayed, the better.

"So," I said. "What's going on with Wendy and Sawyer? Do you know?"

"I don't know the full story," Kai said slowly, "but I do know there are debts he has to pay off. I think he's going to be late now. Well, already late because there's the whole restitution situation—"

The word cut through my inebriated fog. "What?"

"Someone he was coaching a while ago died, and her parents sued him. It's the whole reason we help through work. The whole thing was bull. It was an accident, but there's always got to be someone to blame."

I said nothing.

"He's not perfect, but who is?"

Before either of us could say more, we saw the two of them approaching, walking hand in hand. They stopped at our eyeline. He took his hands in hers and kissed her deeply. My eyes stayed on her as he did. So, they had money problems. Money problems weren't the end of the world. But, restitution, though? Maybe there was something else going on.

Sawyer acknowledged us both first. "Having a good night?"

I nodded. "Yeah."

"Good."

He took Wendy by the hand and led her inside the house.

After a moment, Kai told me he was going inside. I stayed for I don't know how long and watched the stars.

The sky was so clear. There was nothing but the rustle of the wind and the glittering stars to remind me that I was a speck in the grand scheme of things.

.   .   .

THE NEXT MORNING, I woke up to an orange sky. It was supposed to be another perfect day. I put on a fleece and slippers and walked out to the patio. I hadn't been out there for long when I felt a firm hand on my shoulder. It was Sawyer.

"Good morning," he said.

"Morning."

"Sleep well?"

I smiled. "Yes."

He pulled up a seat and scooted next to me. "I'm going to have Leilani take you back as soon as she's awake."

I blinked. "Take me back?"

"You need to go home, Ingrid," he said. "You can't stay here."

I raised my eyebrow at him, confused. "I'm sorry, did I do something wrong?"

"I just need you to go."

My stomach churned as I processed what he was telling me. "What do you mean you need me to go?"

"Ingrid. Don't fight me on this."

He got up and left before I could say more. I racked my brain, thinking of what could have possibly offended him so much that I was being kicked out. It was as if every gut feeling about why it was better for me to isolate was proven right. The second I'd told myself that it was all in my head, this happened. Figures.

Leilani was uncomfortably cheerful that entire morning. I didn't even get to say goodbye to Wendy or Kai before we were practically pushed out the door. We stopped at a McDonalds and got breakfast sandwiches and coffee for the drive.

"Did I do something wrong?" I asked once we were back on the road.

She stared at me blankly. "Don't you have to be back home this afternoon?"

I opened my mouth to say something and then thought the better of it. "Never mind."

"It was nice to meet you," she said in a sing-song voice.

"Yeah," I said.

We didn't speak the rest of the drive. Before long, she'd pulled up to my building and handed me my bag. I watched as her car disappeared, realizing that I'd left the printout of my chapter there. Whatever. I trudged up to my apartment and started crying as soon as I collapsed onto my bed. I still didn't even know what I'd done wrong.

This is why you don't try. Remember that, I told myself.

I didn't think anything of it the first day Wendy didn't show up to work.

By Tuesday, I was worried but not overly alarmed. At lunch, I wrote her a long message apologizing for every-thing. I didn't get a response.

That afternoon, I caught Pidge in the break room.

"Hey," I said. "Do you know when Wendy will be back in the office? I have to talk to her about something."

Pidge clenched his jaw. "Talk to Jacob about whatever you need. Wendy's out."

"Oh. Is she sick?"

"Just talk to Jacob."

By then, people around the office were starting to whisper, but I stayed relatively insulated from it all. I sent her another text. Still, nothing.

On Wednesday, a day before my birthday, detectives came to the office. My heart started to race. I thought for sure that something had happened, and they'd want to talk to me because I was there.

But they came and went, even passing me by as they did.

That night, I came home to find Jenna and her mom sitting in the living room.

"Oh, hey," she said, not taking her eyes away from the TV. "My mom's visiting for the week."

"Sounds good." At one point, I'd have been a lot more frustrated about her not communicating these things in advance, but I was so past the point of caring.

Her mom waved, and as I moved toward my room, my eye caught what they were watching. It was a news report, and I thought I recognized the lake house. Then, I saw the headline.

CONTROVERSIAL AUTHOR, THREE OTHERS FOUND DEAD

"Catch this," Jenna said. "Right in Lake Forest. Some people took poison, and they're all dead."

"What? When did this happen?"

"Last weekend, I think. The maid showed up and found them."

"Just terrible," her mom added.

The screen flashed pictures of Sawyer, Kai, Leilani and Wendy. I went straight into the bathroom and threw up.

I DIDN'T SLEEP at all. I just lay motionless in bed as the previous Saturday morning played over and over in my head. I watched as the clock shifted from 11:59 to midnight, and I officially turned twenty-eight years old.

Eventually, I drifted off and found myself awake at 3:45 in the morning. My thoughts were racing so fast that I had to press my head hard into my pillow so that I didn't faint.

They had to have known what they were going to do when Sawyer kicked me out.

But why?

Why did I deserve to live?

Did I not pass some sort of test?

What did he see—or not see—in me?

Controversial author...

Restitution... the girl that died... I still didn't know anything about that.

All I knew was that in the cold hum of early morning, as the darkness of my room enveloped me, I didn't know what I was or why I was still here.

I was twenty-eight. I didn't know where I'd be by

twenty-nine. So much and so little could happen in a year all the same. But, something Sawyer had told me played over and over in my head. *"You're going to inspire so many people with your words someday."*

Was that why?

It didn't make any lick of sense.

Acknowledgments

As the saying goes, "sometimes, the only way out is through." It may seem ironic that a collection of stories about the senselessness of human nature would help me see its light, but that's been the arc of this process for me.

Connor Fineran, Dee Kannapan, L.E. Medlock and Madi Taylor, not only for your thoughtful feedback on these stories, but for your love and support.

Kaitlynn Flint, thank you for being such an amazing cheerleader.

Nick Muller and Jess Bettis, for letting me read "End of the Century" to you and the rest of the guests at your Halloween party last year.

Mom, for being a captive audience and always encouraging me.

Nell, Natalie, Cassie, Rose, Janet, Madeline, Freya, Oona, Masha and Ingrid are ten women whose paths might never directly cross, but I think of them as kindred spirits, searching for a spark of hope in a dark and uncertain world. As people, that's all we can do.

As a storyteller, my primary goal is to help others feel a little less alone. So, if you've trusted me with that by engaging with my work, I thank you, from the bottom of my heart.

About the Author

Eleanor Wells is a writer, filmmaker and actress, born and raised in Milwaukee, Wisconsin. She graduated from Emerson College in 2017 with a BA in Media Arts Production. She resides in Los Angeles, California, and is the author of *All Our Yesterdays*.

www.ingramcontent.com/pod-product-compliance
Ingram Content Group UK Ltd.
Pitfield, Milton Keynes, MK11 3LW, UK
UKHW041136130325
456102UK00020B/79/J